THE SEAL OF 33

CHRISTOPHER MORTON

GREAT ARCHITECT
PUBLISHING

Published by Great Architect Publishing
Copyright © Christopher Morton 2025

The author asserts the moral right under the Copyright, Designs and Patents Act 1988 to be identified as the author of this work.

All rights reserved. No part of this publication may be reproduced, stored in a retrieval system or transmitted, in any form or by any means without the prior consent of the author, nor be otherwise circulated in any form of binding or cover other than that in which it is published and without a similar condition being imposed on the subsequent purchaser.

This is a work of fiction. Unless otherwise indicated, all the names, characters, businesses, places, events and incidents in this book are either the product of the author's imagination or used in a fictitious manner. Any resemblance to actual persons, living or dead, or actual events is purely coincidental.

ISBN Print: 978-1-0683986-0-5
ISBN eBook: 978-1-0683986-1-2

DEDICATION

This book is dedicated to my late father
Frank Morton, whose love continues to guide
and inspire me every day.

I also dedicate this work in memory of my
devoted proofreader Jacky Mann.

Both true Geordies who enriched the lives of
everyone fortunate enough to know them.

CHAPTER 1

IT was one of those dark freezing nights in Newcastle. A ghostly wind was howling up the River Tyne, as I turn over, the clock strikes three a.m. The soothing patter of rain hits the window and fills the room with a calming rhythm. I find it hugely comforting watching it from my warm bed. As I scroll through YouTube's endless corridors, a peculiar video catches my eye, and it was way past the witching hour. A simple black screen with thirty-three mysteriously hangs in its centre. I'm ready to scroll past when a gravelly voice draws me in with a simple introduction.

"Hello, my name is FRX, and if you are still listening, then you have found this video for a reason."

I listen in closer with anticipation as he begins his speech.

"The things I'm going to divulge will be lost on ninety-nine per cent of people. The magical path is not for everyone.

It's a hard path, but the hardest paths have the greatest rewards. Government and religion have failed us, and science rules the world. The Shadow Advanced Federation, better known as the SAF, is on the rise. They claim to have all the answers to cure disease, end war, and world hunger. This is a smokescreen. Of course, the world's elites have made a deal with artificial intelligence, and they're on the path to destroying the rest of humanity. They are doing everything in their power to end consciousness and true free will."

After a long pause, he pipes up again, "Times are changing, and the darkness is creeping in."

FRX's words paint a world where the powerful play with technology as though they are doing a corporate deal with God himself.

"Over the past decade we have been on the brink of having the answers to cheat death." He stops and gathers his words,

"The quest to be immortal and perfect, to never make a mistake in your life, is madness. Now in 2033, if they are successful, the technological grid will block the universal mind, and humanity will fall into a deep sleep."

His words overflow with a sense of emergency and a deep-seated belief in the web of secrets he was unravelling. As if he alone holds the key to unlocking a truth hidden from the masses. Despite the outlandish nature of his claims, I continue listening, regardless.

FRX shouts out the screen and startles me.

"Well done. If you've made it this far, this is all by design, of course. It's time to wake up and begin your first lesson and find your coven. Your fellow magicians are in every city and corner of the globe. You will know in your heart when you have found them. Join the magical resistance before it's too late."

His final call to join the resistance feels like a joke, yet it resonates somewhere deep inside me before the video cuts out.

A perfect day had flown by, but the cogs in my head were still turning about last night's video. FRX'S message still whispered in my mind; where would I find my coven? I half laugh to myself and try my best to forget about it. It's time to think about tonight.

I run the security for my dad's hospitality empire. He owns all the bars and restaurants in the North Star district of the city. Tonight, I cashed in the golden ticket and took the night off.

My old best friend, Ethan, has begged me to go to a party with him and all I ever seem to do lately is turn him down. For the sake of our friendship, I thought I would make the effort.

It's time to get ready. I cruise through my luxury penthouse in my father's apartment building. I double clap my hands heavily and the lights switch on automatically. The electronic curtains sweep open at the far end of the room, revealing the panoramic views of the magnificent bridges and the beating heart of the city.

I head into the huge wet room, my white teeth gleaming under the bathroom lights, my chest broad and strong with muscle. I dance my pecs left to right to Depeche Mode's *Enjoy the Silence* that's blasting through my sound system, linked to every room.

Looking at my reflection, I'm fit and handsome, but I'm ghostly white. I need a holiday desperately.

I always like to dress smartly and take genuine pride in my appearance. I slip into my crisp Tom Ford navy suit that had been delivered from our family tailor today. I'm wearing it with a military precision ironed white shirt, and a vintage navy paisley tie that I borrowed from my dad but have no intention of returning. I perfectly tie it in a half Windsor knot round my powerful neck and pair it with Grenson brogue shoes that gleam like mirrors. As I finish getting ready, I take one last look in the mirror and can't help but smile at my reflection. I'm ready for whatever Ethan has in store for me.

It's 7 p.m. sharp according to the giant clock in the foyer of my building, Spiral Heights.

As I stand freezing on the curb just outside my entrance, the distant hum of a powerful engine grows closer. Suddenly, Ethan's car roars into sight. Its sleek design catches my attention immediately. It sounds like a beast.

The motor screeches up with blacked-out windows. I don't have to worry; a hitman wouldn't rock up in a camouflage Mercedes S class.

As I peer into the window, it glides down gracefully. Ethan is grinning from ear to ear.

"I knew it was you." I say.

"Get in, then you drip!" Ethan shouts and I jump into the custom-built bucket seat.

"Do you like my new whip?" he asks, as I look around the car.

Ethan's car is a statement of luxury and power, and I'm impressed. Looking around, it's like a spaceship in here, with top-of-the-range leather interior, neon lights and a digital dashboard with that new car smell. It had to be straight out of the showroom.

Ethan flicks on the interior light, illuminating his face and I burst out laughing. "Who butchered your hair, Edward Scissorhands?"

"It's fashion, you prick." he snarls back at me.

"I remember your mam giving you a basin haircut back in the day, but this haircut is on another level."

He doesn't look amused; he cranks up the tune and Sam Fender's *Hypersonic Missiles* nearly bursts my eardrums.

I look to strap myself in as he screams, "What a tune!" the dashboard rattles as he floors the accelerator.

We take off and skid in circles at the end of my street. Buildings flash by us in a blur as we whizz through the city at high speed.

"Where are we off then?"

"South Parade, there's a massive party and they're in need of my services." He shouts over the blasting music.

"We're mixing with the upper classes now, are we?"

"They're my best customers. They've got money to burn."

South Parade is well known as a chic part of the city, popular with the young and trendy crowd.

"I thought we were having a proper catch up, not you taking me on a dodgy drug deal as your backup. You know I want nothing to do with that shit." I'm feeling annoyed already, and the night hasn't even started.

"When did you get so anxious? Just chill out, business will take five minutes. Everything is sorted. It's a straight exchange, then we can have fun at the party. There will be loads of high-end girls you can charm, capeesh?"

I had a feeling this could be a dangerous night. Anything could happen when Ethan was on one.

We approach a mansion beautifully lit up on its own grounds. The gardens and hedges are a work of art. We skid to a halt on the gravel. A Greek God fountain stands proudly in the centre of the drive, and the tranquil sound of the water puts me at ease whilst I wait for Ethan to sort his life out.

"What are you doing in that boot? Have you got one of your ex-girlfriend's tied up in there; you freak?" I joke.

"I'm just sorting the Oscars and Gary Ablett's out."

"Speak English, you weapon."

"The coke and pills. I'll shift the lot in one go. Archie, who owns the gaff, buys in bulk."

"Well, at least you look the part." He flashes me a cheeky grin in response.

He's decked out in a full-length, bright yellow, lightweight Stone Island parker jacket, skinny jeans that complement his oversized Alexander McQueen black and white trainers and an Aquascutum original check overnight bag. The bag is nearly pulling his arms out of their sockets with the contraband he's carrying, but he still swaggers up the drive like Liam Gallagher.

A large, old oak door stands before us with a heavy looking bronze knocker in the shape of a lion's head hanging in the centre.

Ethan bangs the knocker three times with a deafening boom.

I can hear footsteps approaching the door; a well-spoken gentleman says, "Password please."

"I have a dream," Ethan blurts out quickly. There's a long, uncomfortable silence. Ethan shakes his head, confused. The door creaks open a crack, a stone-cold face peers at us.

"It's Ethan, you berk, let us in."

A suave-looking, six-foot, handsome man with slicked back, dark hair and bright blue eyes greets us opening the door. He had to be part of a rowing crew with his barn door shoulders. He had a genuine air of sophistication.

I think to myself, *do not laugh at his pencil-thin moustache*. I still wanted an invitation to this so-called party.

With a wide, cunning grin, he shakes my hand formally.

"Evening, I'm Archie."

"Hi, I'm James, nice to meet you," I reply assertively.

"Please come in. You're stood there like a couple of

vampires waiting for the invitation to enter."

Archie leads us through an elegant hallway with marble floors. A grandfather clock chimes 8 p.m., and Archie turns and scowls at Ethan.

"You're always late. I told you 7p.m., don't you own a diary, you pillock. Please tell me you brought the merchandise in that attractive overnight bag."

"Have I ever let you down?"

"Good man. Come on, follow me." Archie replies.

A black and white chequered floor leads us through a grand dining room with soaring ceilings and elegant antique furniture throughout. Enormous historical oil paintings loom over us on either side. They look like portraits of army generals. Archie had to be from military stock.

"I love the artwork!" I shout from the back.

Ethan pipes up instantly, "It's shite. What happened to pictures of dogs playing pool and poker? Now that was artwork." Archie shook his head in bewilderment.

I wander through his home in awe. I feel like I'm in the presence of someone I can finally relate to. All the windows had black heavy blitz curtains drawn from any prying eyes on the estate. We enter a blood-red archway that's a tad gothic and creepy for my taste.

Archie spins and brightly smiles.

"Welcome to my bunker, boys."

My jaw drops. It's like the great library of Alexandria, with stunning leatherbound books that reach the soaring ceilings. A real woody smell fills the air. It makes me think of a Frank Zappa quote. "So many books, so little time." Archie looks proud of his library, a true sanctum of knowledge,

"Are you an avid reader, James?"

"There are rare hardback books and vinyl that I like.

I've got quite the collection tucked away," I say smugly.

"I'm sure they'll be banned by the SAF soon." Archie gives me a stern, concerned look. He moves one of his oil paintings to the side, revealing an old-fashioned, rusty red, strong looking safe.

"OK, let's get down to business, what's the damage, Ethan?"

"It's sixty grand brother, and I don't want it in old five-pound notes either, you cheap toff."

"You are a crude little man, aren't you?" Archie pulls out a wedge of cash from his safe and stacks it high on the immaculate snooker table to his right. Ethan hands over the merchandise and the exchange is done. That was one drug deal that seemed to go smoothly.

"I think I'll powder my nose," Archie says as he leans in and blasts a six-inch thick line of Peruvian marching powder off the side of the snooker table. He lets out a gasp of fake pleasure,

"This is top gear, Ethan. I can't feel my face. James, can I tempt you?"

I swiftly decline but add, "I'll have a drink though if you have one, please."

I can still hear my dad's voice rattling in my head,

"If I ever catch you with pills or powder, I'll break your legs." Mad Ray's message hit home growing up. I'd hear that rant every weekend as I left the house.

Archie fixes me a rare fifty-year-old expensive whiskey from his vintage globe drinks cabinet. I love the smell of its luxury and elegance and the sound of ice rattling in the glass. I look on at Ethan sampling his own goods like a greedy little pig.

Ethan's like a pocket rocket now, stuffing mounds of cash into his bag.

"I thought you were having a party?" he shouts. "It better

not be a masquerade ball full of devil-worshipping fruits."

Archie raises his voice, "Patience, my boy."

I chug down the whiskey. It makes me shudder from head to toe.

Archie spins to me "James, why don't you look at the golden book in the centre to your right?"

I step closer and look at the title down the spine. I turn with a wide smile. *The Lion, the Witch and the Wardrobe.*

"I love this book."

Archie nods, "Pull it from the top."

I pull down hard. A mechanical lock releases a leather padded door that must be over two feet thick.

"Welcome to Narnia boys!" Archie shouts excitedly.

Ethan whispers in my right ear, "See, I told you I'd take you to a party."

We head down a beautiful, handcrafted wooden spiral staircase. I can feel the vibration pounding in my chest from the music getting louder and louder. I'm getting excited now. Archie punches in the six-digit passcode and pushes open the secret door to Narnia.

A third dimension of smoke, lighting and lasers. The beams cut through the smoke as blazing techno nearly blows the roof off the mansion. Archie shakes my hand and pulls me in for a powerful hug.

"Mi casa es su casa," he whispers and then vanishes into the thick smoke.

Screams of joy roar across the dance floor. Ethan seems to know everyone as we snake through the crowds stomping to the tune. We shake sweaty hands, hug, and kiss stunning girls. This is unbelievable.

"I need a drink, brother!" I scream. Ethan points to a long empty bar in the corner.

"I'll see you out there, bonny lad."

He disappears into the wall of smoke and drumbeats. All the hairs on my body are standing up, everyone seems really friendly.

The long corner bar is quiet. I order an array of cocktails from a talented mixologist. I'm straight into the espresso martinis to bring myself up with a bit of a buzz.

Round two, Amaretto sours are bright and refreshing and make me feel like I'm on holiday.

I nearly drop my drink when I see her at the end of the bar. She looks out of place, in a glamorous Italian Vogue outfit. She's wearing a long, navy blue pencil skirt that shows off her never-ending legs. It's paired with a fitted, crisp white shirt with large shoulder pads and six-inch Louboutin heels, she ticks all the sexy secretary boxes.

She's a goddess.

I feel like I'm levitating in slow motion above the smoke on the dance floor, like an alien spacecraft is beaming me up against my will.

I can't hear the music anymore; time has stopped as I approach her.

The light shines on her perfect features, her beautiful blonde hair is tied up, revealing her ridiculously sexy mouth. Her sparkling blue eyes are like crystalline waters that lap up on a paradise island. She sways side to side with the tune, I'm captivated.

If I had a ring, I would propose now.

She looks me up and down, flashes a cheeky smile and pouts.

"If you're trying to woo me with your best lines, I'm afraid I've heard them all before."

I let out a weird laugh and think, *do you come here often won't cut it.* She's biting her bottom lip, and I move in for the kill.

"Hi, I'm James,"

"Hi, I'm Scarlett."

"Would you like a cocktail?"

"Sure, why not?"

I hand her Ethan's amaretto sour.

"Who are you here with?" She even speaks sexily.

"My friend Ethan."

I point towards the dance floor. You can just make him out. Great, he's got his top off, already drenched in sweat.

She bursts in to laughter.

"Yes Ethan, everybody knows Ethan, he's a good guy." She takes a step closer and clinks my glass.

"Cheers James." She downs the drink in one go like a true professional then looks into my eyes assertively.

"You're a handsome guy dressed to impress. I like your style, maybe you should ask a girl on a date, or is chivalry a lost art these days?"

I let out a nervous laugh. "Of course, where would you like to go?"

"I like a man to take the reins."

I'll have to think fast to impress this beauty.

"OK, I'll hire out Whitley Bay Ice Rink for just the two of us. Do you own skates?"

"Sure," she says eagerly, "I've got a pair tucked away in the garage."

"That's good, you'll break your neck with their rentals." She lets out a perfect laugh.

"We'll skate the night away, then head back to my uncle's restaurant for a midnight feast and see where the night takes us."

"This sounds original, James. I thought you were going to bore me to tears over chicken and rice at Nando's and talk about what you can bench press, but you're funny."

"I know, I have a black belt."

"In what?"

"Banter, Haha!"

"You're sure of yourself, I like that. But unfortunately, it's getting late, I've got work tomorrow and I need to be home by midnight."

"OK Cinderella, give me your number." She slowly steps backwards.

"If you really want this date, you'll find me," she purrs.

The DJ drops Paul Oakenfold's *Southern Sun*, which is a perfect ending to our short acquaintance. I glance after her as she vanishes into the fog. I can't let her slip through my fingers. I won't fret though; Ethan can find her for sure.

My dreaded work phone starts to vibrate in my pocket. So much for my night off. I can just about hear a concerned voice at the end of the line.

"Sorry to disturb you, boss. The Young brothers have got into the bar before the lads started their shift."

"Brilliant, don't worry. I'll be there in forty-five minutes. Keep a lid on it until I get there."

"OK, thank you."

I hang up and make a sharp exit, leaving the party while I switch in to work mode, ready to deal with the trouble ahead.

❖

CHAPTER 2

THE Young brothers run the red-light district on the other end of the city and control the drug trade coming up the River Tyne. They're doing their best to flood the city with drugs.

Ali, Max, and Stan are three ruthless brothers, hellbent on making a name for themselves. They've always been jealous of my family. The Gunner family name is synonymous with Newcastle gangland history. The newspapers call us the Geordie Mafia, but my dad will swear he's just a legitimate business owner who has invested well and manifested his obscene wealth.

I'm lucky one of my dad's drivers is in the area to pick me up. I think it's best to leave Ethan on the dance floor, he looks like he's having too much fun as I sneak away.

I've spent ten years building a reputation on the doors and earnt my stripes from countless brawls. I've never been afraid of anyone, and you get conditioned to fighting on a regular occurrence from the game I'm in.

As the car pulls to a stop I jump out and a sheer wall of noise hits me. Laughter and banter fill the air, and the vibrant lights of the surrounding bars illuminate the night.

The North Star district is blazing with excited visitors as

they line the cobbled streets.

Other cities might be bigger and more glamorous but if you want to party, you'll never find nightlife anywhere like Newcastle. Everybody just wants to have a good time and forget about tomorrow. These are the times we are living in.

I pause for a moment as I approach the entrance to Donavan's. I take a deep breath through my nostrils, exhaling slowly into the chaos surrounding me. Donavan's is my dad's high-end Irish saloon bar, the largest on the strip, with a famous house rock band and freezing Guinness tasting as good as any pint in Dublin. It's always packed with an electric atmosphere; it's my job to keep the idiots out of the bar so people can feel safe and be sure to have a good time.

A group of stunning women pass me by, giving me the once over with bright smiles and fun giggles as I walk in. I can't see the Young brothers. Hopefully, they've left already, and I'll be able to relax.

My right-hand man Jay is holding the fort. Gypsy Jay as he's known, a world champion bare-knuckle boxer who is made of steel. He's old school, with strong values and treats people with respect. Never underestimate his raw power or touch his slicked-back perfect hair. He was serious backup, and I was happy to have him by my side.

"What's happening, Jay?"

"I'm good Jimbo, I'm just hoping for a quieter night than yesterday, if possible."

"Ha, you're in the wrong trade, brother. Who else is on?"

"Big Faruq is doing the rounds, and The Beast is late as usual."

Faruq is a man mountain, over six feet eight inches tall, weighing in at a mighty twenty stone. With short, cropped hair, friendly blue eyes and an iron jaw, his sheer presence is enough to keep any stag party in line.

Come to think of it, I've only seen him throw one punch in all the years I've worked with him, and I think the guy is still in hospital.

He reckons he is ex-special forces, but the truth is starting to creep out now; he didn't even make it through National Service and is now AWOL from the Iraqi army. His mam Sadia is a double diamond and like a pretend aunt to me. I love his family, and they always look after me, inviting me to their never-ending family gatherings.

The Beast is just The Beast. He'll try to sleep with any woman. When he's not being a sex pest though, he knows the job inside out. He's built like a Sherman tank.

The Beast approaches the front saloon door with a wide stupid grin, his tie bursting from his twenty-two-inch solid neck. I'm raging at him but keep my cool.

"You're nearly an hour late, you dickhead."

"I know Jim. I'm sorry I hit traffic."

"You're on the late shift, there is no traffic, you plum. I got here in forty minutes from South Parade. You know I need a full team here in case it goes up. Don't let me down again and lay off those steroids. If you flare those shoulders, you'll rip that new suit off your back and I'm not buying you another one."

The big dope looks puzzled but flashes me a friendly grin.

My crew are there to stop any trouble, not start it, I only hire the best. We all look the business in our matching blue suits. The lads stand strongly on either side of me.

This was one wall you're not bringing down.

Twenty minutes later, the bar's jumping and at full capacity. The Beast is smiling and winking at every woman who walks in. I shake my head.

"You're doing my nut in tonight. You must be on the sex register by now?"

He lets out a deep grunt that I can only presume is his weird laugh.

"It's a numbers game," he replies eagerly. "One of them will fall for me by the end of the night and I must take someone back to mine or I'll not sleep."

"Sounds like a grim system, Beast." Surveying the bar, I continue.

"Jay, hold the fort, Big Faruq will be back soon and I'm away to do the rounds."

I like to run a tight ship and always have one or two men inside.

The house band blasts out *Dreams* by Fleetwood Mac.

You would think thunder and lightning had just struck the dance floor. It was the Youngs kicking off with a couple in the bar corner.

I loosen my top button and slip off my tie quickly, as I snake and weave through the crowd catching snippets of conversations. I exchange brief nods and friendly smiles with the customers so to not cause any panic. Each step brings me closer to the carnage that's about to unfold.

I realise, I've just broken the cardinal rule: never go on the dance floor without your radio for backup.

I tense myself, ready for action. I think the best idea will be to tackle the biggest one first to break the other's confidence.

The biggest of the two is a six-foot, lanky, sunken faced cretin with long greasy hair and yellow teeth that glow under the stage lights. His grubby white denim jacket makes him look like a grade-A sexual predator.

By the time I make it through the crowds, the couple

they were harassing have disappeared, making a lucky escape.

I approach the Young Brothers with a stern, assertive voice.

"Evening gents, can you see your drinks off please?"

The three of them burst out laughing.

"Who's going to make us young'un'? I don't see your dad or uncle anywhere."

I'm getting pissed off now and let it show by raising my voice over the music.

"You need to leave now!" I bark.

The leader stands his ground, giving me a death stare.

"I'm Ali Young. I'm sure you've heard of me. We'll leave when we're ready."

"I know who you are and it's time for you to leave or I'll be making you leave."

"The word on the street is you're good with your hands young'un." He replies.

An uncomfortably long silence fills the air as he glares at me with his evil smile and disgusting teeth.

His head quickly shifts in my direction; I don't give him a chance to mutter another word. Who knows what he's got up his sleeves?

My heart is rapid, adrenalin soars through my body as he lunges directly at me. I quickly fire devastating shots with perfect precision. One, two and a left hook crashes across his jaw, sending him straight to the morgue.

The pathetic frame of the man crumples onto the dancefloor. I can see most of the clientele looked scared, and they back away, giving me at least twenty feet to work my magic.

"Who's next on the cards?"

The two remaining brothers, Stan and Max stand side to side.

Max pushes Stan forward screaming,

"Do him, Stan, do him!"

I take three hops forward and land a jumping front stamp kick to Stan's guts, sending him flying across the tables.

Goodnight, Vienna.

Screams travel across the bar and all the drinks fall and spray the floor with broken glass.

Two down, one brother to go.

I smile as I move swiftly to take Max out. The little rat goes back into his corner.

He has a permanently dense look on his face. He had to have been dropped on his head as a child. Baldy and chubby, with beady eyes and a weak chin that was about to get smashed.

"You'll pay for this," he snarls.

He reaches behind him and pulls out a large lock knife from his wax Harrington jacket.

"I'm going to run this blade through you, you cocky little shit. I'll teach you!"

Who pulls a blade? What a complete coward.

It frightens me for a split second. You see a knife and the best idea is to run, but not on my watch.

I take my suit jacket off slowly, wrapping it round my lead hand to protect me from his blade. The fire exit door swings open six feet behind him. The Beast appears with a petite redhead.

He must have been on his break.

He spots the knife and grabs two bottles of Brown Ale from the table next to him and lunges forward towards Max, smashing them at the side of each of his ears, disorientating him.

Max drops to his knees, releasing the blade and groans at the blood pissing out of either side of his head.

The Beast calmly walks over and swiftly pulls out a

Taser from inside his suit jacket. He blasts him with 50,000 volts directly at the centre of his forehead.

I wish I had a camera. The look on Max's face is priceless.

He's no sooner hit the floor, and The Beast is into me for a bonus.

Gypsy Jay runs through the crowd and shouts,

"The police are coming, quick!"

Ali and Stan pick up their brother Max from the floor. They all look in terrible shape.

Ali snarls at me, "You're going to pay for this. Tell your dad he's dead."

"Piss off back to the red light you pack of nonces," I shout as The Youngs hobble out the rear fire exit.

I wipe my mouth on the back of my wrist. Luckily, it's just sweat. I'd need a rabies shot if it was their blood.

They leave with impeccable timing as the energy of the room changes immediately when an old-school police commander arrives on the scene seconds later. With a distinct air of authority and power, his steady gaze surveys the room, taking in every bit of detail and evidence of his new crime scene. He towers over me and looks the part in his uniform, his Brian Blessed-style voice echoes across the room.

"Who's in charge here?"

I quickly put my suit jacket back on to make myself presentable.

"I am, officer."

"You seem to have had a visit from a rival gang, young man."

A wall of silence falls over the lads.

"Is anyone going to make a statement?"

Once again, silence from everyone.

The commander steps in closer, "Listen, we know you're just doing your job and acted in self-defence. We just need you to make your statement and we can have them all picked up."

"Unfortunately, officer, I do not know who the men are." I know he doesn't believe me.

"OK, have it your way. You're shut down for the night." I let out a groan, my dad will hit the roof.

The commander spins on one heel and marches off. His officers usher the angry crowd out onto the cobbles. One of his messenger boys approaches me with a smug look on his weasel face.

"You have thirty minutes to clear the place, or we'll be back to shut you down for a month. Do you understand?"

"Yes, officer, no problem." I turn to the boys.

"It looks like you all have a flyer. Get everyone out of the main entrance and I'll lock up. Good work Beast, my dad will square you up with a bonus."

I quickly head to my private bathroom to get cleaned up. The freezing cold water brings me back down to earth.

I know I'm a target with my family name, and it won't be long before some new kid in his twenties tries to make his own name and challenge me.

I receive regular death threats. That's why I train so hard, so I'm battle-ready. I felt anxious tonight despite all the training, but I think I deserve a medal for the way I dismantled the Young brothers.

There's a deadly silence as I walk back into the bar, except for the crunching of broken glass under my feet. I step out onto the balcony entrance and quickly look up into the night sky. The distant hum of a military drone hovers directly above me. It's shining its navigation lights on to Donavan's entrance. The distinctive grey and black camouflage outline and bright lights blind me for a moment. Who knows if they are police, SWAT or SAF taking constant footage of me?

They are normally invisible eyes in the sky, but they mean business when they reveal themselves. This is the least of my worries, and I choose to ignore them.

The shutters rattle down the front door as I quickly lock the building up and set the security alarm system.

I set off into the night, flagging a black cab. Let's see what Ethan has in store for me, anything will do to take my mind off this carnage.

I arrive back at Archie's estate just under an hour later. Ethan is waiting for me in the grand lobby.

"Where have you been, you nugget? I was just about to leave."

"I got called into work. Let's just go to mine for a drink."

Trying to find Ethan's camouflage motor in pitch black was comical.

A set of headlights cuts through the trees, blinding us. I put my arm up to cover my eyes, but I feel something is wrong in my gut.

We quickly reach his car as adrenaline courses through my veins. The headlights cast an intense beam that illuminates the gravel path beneath us.

"Who do you think it is?" Ethan says quietly.

"I don't know, brother, but why are we whispering?"

"Strap yourself in tight. I've got sixty grand in that bag and I'm not about to get taxed."

Ethan starts the motor up with a roar and the tyres crunch over the gravel, he keeps his speed low with the headlights off.

The other car heads towards us at increasing speed. I

can just make it out now. It was a burgundy Range Rover Sport with blacked-out windows.

The number plate read YO11 UNG.

I let out a gasp and Ethan quickly turns and looks at me.

"What's wrong?"

"Someone has followed me here. It's the Youngs."

"What did you do?"

"I may have broken a few jaws."

Ethan shrieks with laughter.

"This is no joke, Ethan. We need to bail."

"I know who they are, and I don't fancy getting diced up either."

The Range Rover suddenly flies towards us, the handbrake turning perfectly, gliding along the gravel at the right side of us.

Ali Young leans out his window, he's pointing a double-barrelled shotgun directly at us.

His eyes are wide and glazed and I think, *this is it.* My life flashes before me, dead at thirty with no life experience other than working twelve-hour days for my dad's empire.

My body tenses as Ethan floors the motor and hurtles us forward to safety.

"Take the chase!" I scream.

We fly down the drive, the Range Rover gets smaller and smaller in the rear-view mirror, and a brief sense of relief fills the air.

Then suddenly, jumping through the hedges at 100mph, the Range Rover cuts across the lawns with ease, its four-by-four wheels hot on our tail.

I can see the three of them in the windscreen and they don't look happy.

The gunmen blasts two shots into the rear window and, with a loud bang, they spray us with shards of glass.

My mind is racing and my ears ringing. We are so lucky we haven't been hit.

Glass is flying everywhere.

Ethan flicks up a plastic square next to the gear stick and screams, "Come on!"

He hits the switch.

Nitric oxide screams through the air as my head jolts back with whiplash force and the speedometer flashes 150 mph.

The dark trees of the forest disappear behind us. I feel the panic leave my chest, I breathe deeper and deeper, bringing my eyes back into focus.

The wind howls through the huge shotgun holes into the rear. My body is numb. I don't know if it's due to shock or the freezing cold.

"See, you took the piss out of my car and once again I save the day." Ethan bursts out laughing.

"Just get us home please," I grumble.

We drive at high speed through the pitch black and into the night. We take another slip road onto the A1 motorway. I knew then we had made it to safety.

We enter the underground garage of my apartment building and skid in a screech of brakes to a violent stop. The doors burst open to shards of glass pouring onto the garage floor like glittering conflict diamonds. Ethan slams his door with anger. "Well, my new motor is a write-off."

"I'll get it sorted at my dad's garage. Just hurry. We need to get out of sight."

We run to my private lift. As I turn to look over my shoulder, Ethan's following me, taping a bulletproof vest around him that he'd pulled out of his boot.

I jam my keys into the lock to release my private lift doors.

We reach the top floor of the apartment building, directly to my penthouse.

Walking into the warmth, I slam the door shut behind us, locking the centre, top and bottom security bolts. The door is made of ten-inch steel and wood, it was designed to withstand a small army to break it down.

"Alexa, play some Northern Soul," I demand.

The lights illuminate the entire apartment.

I quickly run to the window and check the street below. There are no Youngs, or drones and I need a drink to take the edge off.

I turn and let out a light-hearted chuckle that fills the air with a sense of warmth, looking at Ethan standing there wearing a bulletproof vest three sizes too big for him.

"Where did you get that, a second-hand army and navy store?"

"Funny guy, I must have lost a load of weight, it used to fit me."

"You're safe here, you cracker. Take it off. My dad has this place boxed off. It's like Fort Knox. There's security at the front and even a helicopter pad on the roof. I'll order the family chopper and disappear to my grandparents' holiday home in the Glencoe mountains."

I think I've won Ethan over as he takes off the vest.

An escape plan to the Scottish Highlands sounds like a treat at the minute.

"What happened to your grandad? You never talk about him anymore."

"You're not allowed to talk about him. That's the rule my dad has set, so I just keep quiet." I reply sombrely.

I can't believe he brought my grandad up after the night we've had.

"I know they gunned my grandad down. They were

waiting in the shadows as he left his home. High-powered motorbikes rode past and chopped him down with a spray of bullets. I hope someone was looking out for him upstairs. He vanished into thin air, and he's not been seen for over five years. I miss him dearly and I'd rather not talk about the past tonight." I continue, "Your patter is always the same. Remember when, remember when, don't you know it's the lowest form of conversation?"

He lets out a deep snigger that echoes through the room. An insidious shriek that leaves the room with an uncomfortable tension.

"You should be honoured to be in my company. We hardly see each other anymore. Which bathroom shall I use?"

"Through the apartment, the last door on the right."

The kitchen light shows his squinting, bloodshot eyes with a hint of yellow and black rings underneath as he shuffles off to the bathroom.

I know he's struggling, and he can't hide it from me. He's not the man I grew up with. He's fallen into the abyss of the drug world, and I barely recognise him.

Ethan could have been a prize-fighter, as he lived and breathed the fight game back in the day. His ego took over, though. He started partying on the weekends, then thirsty Thursday crept in, and before you knew it, he was on one seven days a week. That's when he became unreliable and ruined his boxing career.

He's trapped in his past and has firmly anchored himself there, as that's all he talks about—the "good times," he would say.

He returns from the bathroom, trying to hide the tremendous pain behind his eyes. I don't have the heart to get into his financial situation or his spiralling drug habit, not tonight. I want to let off some steam, not sit in my kitchen in a full-blown counselling session while he is high as a kite on whatever he's been shoving up his nose in my bathroom. He rubs his hands excitedly.

"What have you got to drink in here?" Looking back at me confused after opening the fridge. "Steak fillets, ham, and Pease pudding? Who are you, Hannibal Lecter?"

"There's Grey Goose in the freezer. Just grab a bucket of ice and we're good to go."

He always used to be a magic ingredient to any party, and I forgot how close we used to be.

Things turn to business, though, as we proceed to forget the drama of the Young brothers and become more intoxicated.

Ethan's face lights up. "We should set up together, brother."

"What do you mean?"

"I've got a couple of business opportunities that could work."

I lean back in my chair with my hands behind my head.

"Let's hear them then."

With his wide grin, he sets the scene.

"OK, there's a container coming in from China. High-end AI latex sex dolls that moan and groan and talk dirty to you in an American accent."

"That sounds grim."

"They're all ringers for Jennifer Lopez, proper sexy and worth ten grand a piece. My man at the North Shields docks is shifting them for two grand."

"OK, what's the catch?"

"They have a minor fault."

"Which is?"

"They're all cross-eyed. Doubt anyone will notice, though."

"Awful idea, what else have you got?"

"OK, you'll like this one better. Let's get into the stolen art game. I've got a solid contact from over the water. He's got a new oil painting that's red hot and he needs to shift it this month. It's a real Leo Da Vini or something."

"You mean Leonardo da Vinci you fool."

"I don't know, I didn't do art in school, did I?"

"You didn't do anything at school other than play cards and drop acid. I guarantee, if your man reckons he's got his hands on the missing Mona Lisa he's full of shit. I'd hand it back in anyway, art needs to be in a museum not locked away in some nonces hidden vault. A little piece of advice Ethan, stick to what you're good at, hijacking cases of wine and designer jackets, capeesh!"

I continue sarcastically, "Because of your awful presentation, I'm out."

Ethan jumps up, furiously.

"I knew you would treat this like *Dragon's Den*, you dickhead. Hear me out. We'll make a good lump of cash on both."

"When you've got something solid, I'll invest, but since you've turned up to the Den high on drugs and mortal drunk with no forecast or concrete plan, I'm out."

A warm smile cracks across his face, it creates a meaningful connection between us.

"You're a shit house and you love to wind me up."

He heads over to the panoramic window and looks up at the sky.

"It's a full moon tonight, Jimbo. That's why you've had all that bother."

I turn and say, "Would you care to explain how the moon nearly got me killed tonight?"

"It's a proven fact that a full moon as big as this one, makes people into raving loons and you've been a magnet for them tonight."

"Once again, you've proven to me that you need to lay off the powder. My friend, it's making you delusional."

He chose to ignore me, continuing to gaze out the window.

"Do you think you'll ever settle down with the house on the hill and get out of this posh apartment?"

"You slate me, but you feed off the same energy of the city and as time flies before we know it, we'll be in our fifties. Since you mention it, I may have finally found someone on the dance floor tonight. Her name is Scarlett, a smoking hot blonde with lethal banter, a rare find."

"Have you been saving up for a ring?"

"No, I just think there was an actual connection." I say with a smug smile.

"You change birds every calendar month, bonny lad." Ethan said, slamming his whiskey glass on my countertop.

He had me all wrong. I hate it when someone knew a version of you ten years ago and they think you're the same person now.

❖

CHAPTER 3

I feel like I've been hit by a truck and have no intention of making any sudden movements. Feeling nauseous, the thought of vomiting on my new silk sheets is not on my list of things to do today.

One eye opens, then the other. The ceiling spins like a fairground waltzer.

I lay on my back for a few moments, confused and trying to piece together last night. Ethan had bolted and left me in the mess of my apartment.

It had to be midday; the sun was high in the sky and the light shone all the way through the apartment. I feel like a creature of the night, if the sunlight reaches me, I'd surely burn.

Coming in thick and fast, the sound of pitter-patter echoes across the oak chequered flooring. My dog, Nipper pelts towards me with his tail wagging a hundred miles per hour.

He springs directly onto my crotch, and I let out a high-pitched scream with a definite harsh taste in my mouth that could be vomit. He runs straight up my body, landing like a tonne weight on my head, chewing my ears to let me know I'm part of his pack.

I love how excited he is to see me every morning. He is

the most handsome Miniature Bull Terrier you've ever seen, a true Crufts champion with his shiny black coat, perfect little baby white socks, and cheerful grin.

He finally calms down and curls up like a baby fox next to my ribs. I lay there and rub my eyes again, instantly feeling the impending doom. I glance at my phone on the bedside cabinet, I've truly done it here. I'd put the phone on silent mode last night and it was now 1p.m. My dad was at the top of the screen with eight missed calls.

I jump out of my skin as it lets out a loud vibration in my hand but answer as though nothing is wrong.

"Hi, I'm literally getting in the car now. How are you?" There's a deadly silence on the other end.

"Dad, are you there?"

Brilliant, the line goes dead. It was time to face the music, and I knew I was in deep shit.

I pull on my maroon Stone Island rain mac and grab a freezing bottle of Lucozade out of the fridge to take the edge off this blazing hangover.

Giving Nipper a quick cuddle and a kiss I throw on a pair of Ray Bans to hide my tired eyes, dart out the door and head down to the garage.

Ethan's car had magically disappeared and there wasn't a shard of glass in sight. My dad must have seen the cameras and had it towed.

I head over to my parking spot, jump in and rev up my BMW sports car, heading out of the city, speeding up the A1 Motorway towards my father's estate.

The sun is high in the beautiful blue sky as I floor the accelerator through the winding, narrow, unforgiving country roads.

The open farmer's fields and rolling hills whizz past as I get lost in the lush scenery.

Only the elite could live in this prestigious area. Every house has its own unique design, with sprawling estates and a countryside feeling only fit for the Land Rover and tweed suit mob.

Being out in nature brings a sense of freedom and I quickly forget about my hangover and put it behind me. The large, magical, wise old trees give way as I drive to my father's estate.

My dad's home security was over the top. I would call him paranoid; he would call it comfortable.

I slow down to 10mph and approach the large gothic gates with huge stone angel pillars on either side. They always make me feel as though they're judging me.

The gates slowly creep open and my car spins on the gravel, driving up through the estate. The lawns are immaculate, with perfect stripes like a black and white Newcastle United football strip.

A fleet of Rolls Royce Phantoms gleam in the sun. I park up next to them and jump out.

I'm sweating now as I approach the house.

Classic Raymond Gunner. He could be as cold as ice when he wanted to be, and he never made small talk.

Everything was business in his eyes.

He's standing tall and proud at the top of his stone stairs. He's dressed in a tailored black suit with a slight flare on the trouser, alligator leather Cuban heels, a white shirt and a black paisley cravat tied perfectly around his slim neck.

His daily morning ritual is jumping out of bed to two hundred press-ups as soon as he wakes up. He's always had a strong long frame and been obsessed with his looks, with short-cropped styled hair, a designer beard and arctic bright blue eyes.

He was one of the few men in my life I'd always tried to emulate. He was immaculate and always drummed that into me growing up.

"Your clothes are important son; they give you an advantage, so always dress to impress."

His black Great Dane, Atlas, stood to his left and his white Great Dane, Hermes, to his right, guarding over him. They look excited to see me but dare not move from his side until he gives the command. They were highly trained by my dad's old friend from the Special Air Service who said they could kill on command. I didn't believe it for one moment, they were loveable, clumsy giants.

The tone of his voice stops me in my tracks when I reach the top of the stairs.

"You cost me eighty grand last night." His voice is harsh.

"I know Dad. I'm sorry, the Youngs got into the bar."

"Why was it your concern? It was your night off." I'm in a daze, listening to him hand it to me.

"Son, you're a liability, not to mention the money you cost me. You don't realise how dangerous you are. You can't hit normal folk with your capabilities. You're going to kill someone one of these days."

"I wish I did!" I shout.

"What are you talking about, you fool? I'm building this empire for you."

"You know for a fact, that the Youngs shot grandad."

"Leave your grandad out of this. The Youngs are not my concern, running a successful family business is."

I'm furious now. "All of their hits have had the same pattern using machine gun motorbikes. It's their calling card."

"That's not proof you imbecile."

"They're going to make a move and try to muscle in on the North Star, or are you too blind to see it? They could be even planning Uncle Crow's execution."

He raises his voice above mine, "Your uncle can look after himself. We are a legitimate business. I'm not part of that world."

He clenches his fists tightly. I can tell I've hit a raw nerve by the veins bulging in his temples bringing up Grandad. I quickly change the subject.

"Where's my mam?"

"Where do you think? She's at the villa."

Newcastle was far too cold for her now and she only came home when she needed to.

My mam was a glamorous, eccentric painter who loved nothing more than to entertain friends and family at the family villa in Marbella, Spain.

"At ease," my dad grumbles and heads into the house.

The dogs pelt towards me, bouncing along with crazy excitement. Their eyes sparkle as they pounce on me, licking either side of my face. It seems they're the only ones happy to see me these days at this house. I truly love my four-legged friends.

I hold my tongue to save any further argument. The Youngs are out of control. If my dad doesn't react to their disrespect from last night, they'll think we've gone soft and make their move.

He returns and drops a bulging overnight Louis Vuitton checkered bag at my feet.

"Take this to your uncle. You know the dance and don't mess it up."

I had to pick up a bag of money for my uncle every month. It was his pocket money from his investments in my dad's business.

Atlas and Hermes trotted back to my father's side. "You behaved like a lunatic, so you must live with the consequences." He says coldly and calmly.

"What do you mean?"

"You're on paid leave. You will keep a low profile until I clean this mess up."

"Hold on, I run the North Star. You said you wouldn't get involved, the boys work for me."

"Son or no son," he snarls, "I am your father and the head of this family. You will do as you're told. Now, piss off out of my sight."

He turns swiftly and marches off with his dogs firmly at his sides.

I'm totally shocked. I've just been sacked by my own dad.

It's taken me ten years to get the North Star district running like clockwork. All that hard work for nothing. If he thinks I'm going to wait by the phone for him, he's sadly mistaken.

The overnight bag feels like a fifty-kilogram dumbbell as I load it into my boot. I turn and look back at the immense house and can't relate to anything anymore. I'm done.

I take off at speed, winding through the hills and valleys back to the city. I approach the North Star district looking in my rearview mirror to make sure I'm not being followed.

My stomach is in knots carrying this amount of unexplained hard cash.

There's bright yellow tape cornering off Main Street and four imposing military vehicles line up ahead. Their blue lights flash with silent sirens. In the middle of all this mayhem is Ethan. His face is filled with fear as he's roughly marched to a vehicle by what looks like SAF soldiers in military clothing and SAS masks.

I brake gently to not draw attention to myself. I cruise into a parking space to hide behind a large builder's van and get a better view.

It's a scary sight to watch. They mean business.

I figure it's best to sit and watch from a distance. They could throw the book at him. This is his third strike with his previous brushes with the law.

I quickly ring my Uncle Crow as he always knows what to do in these situations. Sickness coils in my stomach as the phone just rings off.

"You took your time answering." I say after trying again.

"What's up, nephew?"

"I'm watching Ethan getting carted off by the SAF."

"I know, they're looking for anyone associated with him, they're hitting the district hard. You need to get on your toes, ditch the motor and I'll send a driver to pick you up at your place in thirty minutes."

I'm nervous he already knows they'd banged Ethan up. Uncle Crow has got the entire city on his payroll. I continue to watch the parade, A fit-looking beauty in a leather jumpsuit bangs on top of the roof of the lead vehicle and it roars away through the North Star district.

A stream of blue lights whizzes past, and I quickly crouch down, hiding from them. I fight to keep my hands from trembling, gripping the steering wheel.

After I wait an agonising 10 minutes the coast is clear. I head back to my apartment building; the flashing blue lights are long gone.

The Crow's driver stands waiting in the parking garage as I arrive. I quickly ditch the motor and load the cash into the driver's boot, jumping into the back seat, hiding behind the tinted windows.

We travel at speed through the city and across the Tyne Bridge. Looking down, I can see gunboats patrolling up and down the peaceful river.

My Uncle Crow is the head man in Newcastle, a serious gangster steeped in mystery. He is also a phenomenally successful financier.

It was well known that if you couldn't go to the bank to lend money, you went to The Crow. He had real money on the street and a chain of legitimate businesses. The police never gave him any trouble, he had them in his pockets all the way to City Hall.

We arrive at Oyster Soul, The Crow's famous seafood restaurant overlooking the River Tyne. Stepping through the modern chic entrance, the river provides a soothing backdrop, complementing Oyster Souls' perfect ambiance. The polished wooden floors lead me through pure luxury, with huge windows offering a beautiful view of the calm waters, bringing me a sense of peace.

I enter the restaurant to a warm greeting.

"James, my boy!" He shouts.

Once again, he never lets you down with his fashion, dressed in a deep purple suit handmade by Savile Row's tailors. He has a powerful jaw and high cheekbones, wearing a fedora hat that hides his piercing grey eyes. His style is amazing.

He pulls me in for a powerful hug and I hang on to him a bit too long, as I've missed him so much.

"The restaurant is something else, uncle, it's pure class."

He lets out a light-hearted laugh.

"It's a white elephant, but it will always stay open whatever the cost. I love being close to the river, it helps me chill out, plus I need somewhere I can entertain and hold court. You look well, young man," he says in his deep, local

Geordie accent, "but I can see there is something troubling you." I look around the restaurant and it's deadly quiet.

"Don't worry, you can talk openly here." He replies sensing my unease.

The waiter arrives with bottles of premium quality Sauvignon Blanc and a seafood platter fit for the gods. We take a seat, and I chug back the crisp wine and explain my dilemma.

"The SAF have arrived, and Ethan has been arrested. My dad basically just sacked me for dismantling The Youngs last night at the bar and the list goes on, uncle."

He throws his head back and roars with laughter.

"It sounds like you've had a busy couple of days. Let us toast and drink to The Gunner family."

Our glasses clink and to be honest, I'm feeling at ease just sitting in his presence. The seafood platter looks amazing, with fresh crab and lobster and a vast bed of oysters.

"Dig in, young man. The oysters are from Lindisfarne, the absolute best."

I roll up my sleeves, pull up the platter of oysters and start knocking them back like shots of tequila. Uncle Crow has his own language that flows like poetry.

"General Saturn is holding a conference in town tomorrow and afterwards at St James's Park. He's trying to drum up support in the North. London was the first to fall. They now call it the Stone City. Everyone is a Grey down there."

"What's a Grey?"

"It's when they shut off your aura and your connection to the universe has gone. You've lost your soul to oblivion. Your mind and soul are gone, leaving behind an empty shell of a body called a Grey. The masses are now fast asleep, only driven by ego and material things, easy to control and manipulate."

He's lost me now. He might as well be talking in riddles. I nod away whilst devouring the seafood platter.

"I never thought they would get this far north, and it boils my piss." He slams his hands down on the table with an almighty bang.

"Do you not realise the SAF wants to lead the world into a deep sleep?"

This rings a bell from the video I'd found the other day on YouTube.

"Another bottle of vino, please waiter!" He shouts.

We are well into the second bottle when Ethan becomes the topic of conversation.

"Didn't I always tell you growing up, show me your three closest friends and I'll show you your future?" my uncle said. "I'm proud of you for distancing yourself from Ethan over the last few years. You've kept your circle of real genuine friends small. Three real friends will always outweigh one hundred fake ones. Remember that."

"Yes, uncle, what should I do about Ethan?"

"Ethan is gone."

"How do you mean gone?"

"He's dead. If he worms his way out of jail, he's dead. If he gets a lengthy stretch, he's dead. I found an anomaly in his lending. He was into me for three hundred large when I dug deeper."

I nearly spit my wine out onto the table as he continues.

"He fabricated a story saying some posh kid called Archie still owed him most of his bill, and he was good for it. You look shocked. Spit it out, I know you know something."

"I saw Archie pay him the cash with my own eye's uncle."

"So, there you have it. He's as trustworthy as a box of snakes."

I couldn't get a word in edgeways. My uncle was going to town on Ethan now. "If he's making clandestine deals with the SAF to earn his liberty and giving up information about The North Star district, he will pay dearly."

He flashes me a crazy stare, gulping down half a glass of wine.

"So, it seems he's left you with a bit of a conundrum young man."

"He knows the dance, Uncle. He won't talk. Please don't have him killed. He's just lost the plot from the drugs. I'll get him cleaned up and help to come up with a solid plan to pay your money back."

He pauses for a while, thinking about it while rocking back and forth in his chair.

"OK, if he gets out with no grief, he has sixty-six days to raise my cash, or he'll be swimming in the Tyne. This is on your toes, James. If word gets out on the street that I've been soft with him, then nobody will pay their debts, so don't let me down. Do you get me?"

"I get you."

"Anyway, enough talking about that clown. What's been happening in your life? More wine waiter please!" he shouts again.

It looks like we're on one now.

"I just want out of the game. I've worked non-stop and now I can't relate to anything anymore. I'm burnt out, whilst my dad sits back in his castle, and I make him a fortune every night."

My uncle lets out an enormous sigh.

"You've kept your head down and put in the graft and earned your stripes. I would take that as a fantastic omen.

You must be sitting on a fortune, young man."

"I'm doing OK, but I'm just sick of my dad. He can be such a heartless bastard, sorry uncle, I'm just stressed out."

He leans in with a soothing voice,

"Your dad and I were raised as heathens and we do our best to blend into society, although it's been tough for me with my hedonistic lifestyle. Your dad just hides out the way behind his gigantic walls in the woods.

He continues wisely. "I understand you have a dark side, and it runs through all of us. You are becoming self-aware, and you will recognise your shadow. It holds all the parts of yourself that you don't want to admit to having."

"Sorry about before, uncle, I just get carried away."

A warm smile cracks across his strong face creating a meaningful silent connection between us.

"That's just your ego. Nothing wrong with a bit of ego. Drink up, young man. That's the most expensive Italian wine you can get your hands on."

"So why did they used to call my dad Mad Ray?"

"I doubt your dad would want me to divulge what he used to get up to back in the day. Everyone has a past. Just don't let it define who you are today."

I stare at him with his perfectly strong, weathered looking face bent over his plate of demolished seafood, without looking up, he said, "You're just out of line. You need to balance your system. Earth, air, fire, and water are all part of you. Once you're grounded, then make your move, young man. I'm going to put these oysters to some good use. I've got a couple of Eastern European beauties on the go."

"Thanks for the meal and the advice."

He laughs, clasps his arm around my shoulder and whispers,

"You're from a very special family James; all will be revealed to you soon. You make no harsh decisions in your life when you're out of line, just have some fun. Do you want my driver to take you home?"

"No, I'm good thanks, I could do with the fresh air."

I respect how my uncle has lived his life on his terms, and I've always taken his sound advice. He's been my other mentor my whole life. I just need to find the answers in his riddle.

The wine has gone to my head as I head over the Tyne Bridge. The breeze coming off the river is so harsh it's making me shiver from head to toe despite my lightweight mac. There's a running joke, that people from Newcastle don't own coats and always brave the cold without one.

Marching towards the end of the bridge, SAF military boats are anchored all the way up the river. Drones fly high in the sky, spying on the city.

The only thing I'm interested in is getting a good night's sleep and cuddling up to Nipper.

The weekly Quayside market is happening tomorrow, and I want to add some records to my collection. I keep my head down and head back to Spiral Heights.

I'd just arrived at my apartment door when my phone vibrated. It was a long number I didn't recognise.

"Hello?"

The voice catches me off balance.

"Jimbo, it's Ethan, I'm ringing from Durham jail," he sounds happy and on top form.

"What the hell happened?"

"I was in the wrong place at the wrong time and got pinched. They've got me on conspiracy to supply Class A drugs. I can't talk on this line if you know what I mean. They've got nothing on me. I just had a large sum of money

I was carrying at the time that I can't explain."

He continues quickly, as though his time is running out.

"I need a favour, and this is the last one I'll ever ask for. You know who I need you to talk to. I know he can get to me in here. I'll just leave that to your imagination. I'm on borrowed time, brother. Nobody is picking up. I've been blanked by everyone. You're the only one I can count on to help me."

"I've already spoken to him. He's sent a car for me for a sit-down tonight, and you've left me in a right pickle." There's a long pause and Ethans voice changes.

"I'm so sorry, the drugs have clogged my mind up with what I've been doing. I've lost the plot; I honestly feel like I've cracked my mind into tiny pieces."

"You've been living in chaos and you're in deep, Ethan. We've got time on our side now, I've sorted it." I reply.

There's a deadly silence on the other end.

"Are you still there?" I ask.

A sigh of relief comes over the phone. I believe in karma and always see the good in people, so I gave Ethan one more chance.

"What's the plan then brother?"

"Don't worry, this is just a situation you're in, it's not your life. Don't do anything stupid. I'll pull my money together and we can open a Northern Soul bar. I'll be able to play my records, and you can help run the place and chip off the debt."

"OK brother," he sounds determined. "Thank you, so much. Honestly, I couldn't see a way out of this. I knew I could count on you."

I had to stay strong for him, but I couldn't imagine being in his shoes.

"Get yourself cleaned up in there, get fit and keep your head down and I'll see you soon."

"I love you, kid!"

"I love you too." I reply and hang up.

I knew he'd hit rock bottom in there and that's the only way he could climb back up – a short stint in jail, could be what he needs. It's one shady all-inclusive hotel he doesn't need to pay for when he checks out.

I lay comfortably on my bed with my best little buddy curled up at my side, seeking some love and attention. I keep thinking about the YouTube video, what I found and what it had revealed. As Bob Dylan once said, "The times, they are changing, and this year had to be the strangest year I've ever lived."

Although the world feels like it's spinning the wrong way, I know the universe is trying to tell me something.

I just have to find out what.

Nipper lets out a heavy sigh and we breathe into a perfect rhythm, spiralling into a deep sleep.

❖

CHAPTER 4

I sneak out the fire exit at the side of my building, looking over both shoulders to make sure I'm not being followed by the Youngs. The coast is clear, so I head uptown.

Planning my day ahead, I think I'll drive through The North Star to pick up my things from Donovan's, now I'm under house arrest from my father. I'll then head to the Quayside Market, as this is my normal routine, and I'll hopefully get my hands on some rare Northern Soul records.

Gunboats and people carrier boats rock silently, stretching along the pier of the River Tyne. The SAF has landed with plenty of muscle to flex.

Historically, General Saturn had never been seen in public like this. He's one of the richest men in the world and uses his money and power to build the sleeping giant – The SAF Corporation.

I've heard some real horror stories, and he's been labelled a total psychopath who loves to get his hands dirty. If you cross The General, you're never to be seen again. Hundreds of SAF employees had mysteriously disappeared and a long list had supposedly committed suicide.

Crowds begin to gather in the bustling streets. It was like match day when Newcastle football team played at home, you literally couldn't move with people from all walks of life.

With each passing moment the city streets seem to quieten with anticipation. The sun shines through tall office buildings and bounces off the gigantic screens that appear to have been erected throughout Newcastle overnight. As the screens flicker to life, General Saturn's face appears.

I hear a stern voice in the wind that also booms throughout speakers in every corner of the city.

"Good day people of Newcastle."

"I am General Saturn, the founder of The SAF Corporation."

I stop in my tracks to watch the screen outside of Grey's Monument, and I listen intently to his speech.

"Thank you for coming out on this beautiful day to hear about our exciting proposal. We are here to build support for the human upgrade. The world will align with our project, and we are remarkably close to having the technology that will put our mortality in our hands." His voice heightens with excitement, "Wouldn't you want to live forever and download your own soul?"

A Mexican wave of cheers travels across town from the brainwashed.

"With our full country signing up for our program, Britain will be great again, a true superpower ruling the land and sea. Let us step into this new era together."

He just keeps repeating the same shit over and over, mesmerising the crowds. It feels like a Nuremberg rally to me. Hitler's rise to power was in 1933. I'm now standing one hundred years on, and I get a sick feeling in my stomach. I don't trust science; I trust history and feel they could lead us down the same path.

I quickly snake through the crowd as he continues,

passing heavily armed guard after guard. The most frightening thing about them is their dead eyes under their military masks.

His obvious intent is to crush any resistance as quickly as possible and land in town with a serious show of force, frighten any normal folk into submission and sign their souls away.

All I can feel now is negative energy from the entire crowd. They've been well and truly hoodwinked by this outfit, and I need to bail.

He's still barking out his demands with deafening noise booming from his microphone and surrounding screens, making me feel disoriented. There's a darkness in his eyes that feels alien and void of all empathy. He looks to me like a cold, calculated killer I want no part of, and it's time for a sharp exit.

My marching feet echo through the winding cobbled streets as I pick up pace, moving away from the sea of strange, hypnotised faces. Sunlight filters through the gaps between the buildings, leading me away from Grey's Monument to the safety of my BMW. I take off, blasting through town at high speed, cutting through traffic like a Formula 1 driver.

I feel a bit of relief getting away from the mass crowds and the enormous screens until I see the military vehicles lined up outside of Donovan's bar. It's as if time stands still as I'm transfixed on the rhythmic whirling of the rotating silent blue lights.

I screech up and storm into the entrance, but I'm stopped in my tracks by the sheer beauty of the woman in front of me.

Her long, straight, shining black hair travels down her back to the arch of her spine, with dazzling emerald, green eyes shining through her youthful face. She's wearing a military tactical leather jumpsuit that complements her berserk figure. She stares into my eyes for half a second too long, then glances away, flicking her hair to the side,

"Are you Mr. James Gunner?"

"I am, and I know who you are. You're a long way from home?"

"I am Amora Saturn, and this is my brother Crowley."

He's a lean and powerfully built man who could give me some trouble.

"We're putting new sanctions in the North Star district, and all premises will be closed by 10 p.m."

"You're going to ruin our business!" I shout. "This place doesn't fill up till after 10 p.m."

"You should work with us, not against us. I've heard some fascinating stories about you, James. You are on the rise, ditch the fools that are dragging you down and join us, there is room at the table for you."

Two seconds later, she shows me her other side and her tone sharpens.

"You'll find out soon enough whose side you should be on."

It twists me with rage, my jaw clenches tight, as do my fists. Before I even open my mouth, Crowley moves swiftly across the bar.

"Silence," he hisses, lunging at me with his foul, hot breath. "I used to break guys like you in at the SAF Academy. Maybe I should make you my special little bitch."

I look straight into Crowley's hard eyes with a death stare. He pulls away and breaks eye contact first, so I know he was full of shit.

I raise my voice sternly. "Listen, until we get the sanctions in writing, business will continue as usual so, please piss off out of my bar."

Amora's eyes turn hard and cold and they march off in a hurry without a word.

All I want to do now is forget about these lunatics and head to the Quayside Market.

An hour passes, and as I arrive at the waterfront, brightly coloured canopies stretch along the promenade for miles to see. Laughter fills the air as the bustling market never fails to charm.

The market is a meeting place for locals, holidaymakers, musicians, artists, families and friendly faces as usual. The smell of the food trucks entice me as I bounce along the river front. I can hear Northern Soul music traveling in the gentle wind. My favourite record stall is just up ahead, and my mood changes instantly.

Approaching the stall, cutting through the crowd, I catch a whiff of spicy cinnamon. The air is filled with cigar smoke. I'd know that smell anywhere.

It always reminds me of going to the Tyneside Cinema with my uncle Crow. He used to take me when I was little to see all the classics every Saturday morning at 9 a.m. without fail, and we took turns each week choosing the movie.

He brought me up on a steady diet of westerns. His choice, of course.

Some things I was deeply concerned about when I was growing up were Comanche Indians and quicksand, and these weren't common in the East End of Newcastle.

He suddenly appears from behind a market stall looking immaculate, draped in a green tweed full-length gentlemen's mac, buttoned up high with a pristine tipped beige fedora, that just showed his cunning smile.

I can see devilry in his eyes, he's always up to mischief. He has a way of knowing things other people didn't and was always two steps ahead. His face lights up as I approach.

"James, my boy," he pulls me in for a powerful hug. "What's happening?"

"I've just been grilled by The SAF at the bar. They were trying to pressure me to join them."

He lets out a long sigh, "They're approaching anyone with influence in the city. Just keep your head down and ignore them. They're only here for another three days."

"You should've seen them in town trying to drum up support from the locals. It was like a Nazi rally."

"I know James I was there; follow your gut, the times — they are changing. What records are you looking for?"

"I'm not sure, but I get a feeling I'm about to get relieved of all my cash from Dunc."

Duncan is a rare record dealer with a lean, muscular physique and is short in stature. His face tells many stories. He always dresses smartly, and today he is wearing a fitted Ben Sherman maroon checked shirt with the top button fastened and a navy classic Crombie Mac. He crops his hair very short, and he knows his music but doesn't do small talk.

He greets us with a friendly smile, "Afternoon gents, what can I do you for?"

"Northern Soul of course."

"I've got just the record for you, and I've been holding onto it for a few days."

The Crow steps in, tipping his fedora upwards to make eye contact with him. "Make sure you give him a good deal Dunc, he's family."

He quickly rummages through a metal box.

"Ah, here it is." He sighs, "The best record on the stall and, to be honest, my favourite record of all time, Johnny Mae Matthews," handing me a white sleeve in pristine condition.

Gazing at the sleeve, I half laugh.

"Quite ironic, it's called I Have No Choice." He just cracks me a wide smile in response.

"What's the damage then?"

"I'll take two grand for it this morning. Who knows what it will be worth tomorrow?"

I flip the white sleeve over and there is a message in deep red ink.

The Coven requests you, Holy Island Abbey, July 12th at 7 p.m.

It sends shivers up my spine. Glancing around, I check to see if I catch anyone's eye from the onlookers.

How can this be such a coincidence? The YouTube video I found the other night said to look out for the magical resistance from The Coven. I don't know whether to feel happy or scared.

I found it creepy.

"What's up? You look like you've seen a ghost."

"I'm sound, uncle." Shaking my head, I pull the wedge from my wallet and hand the two grand to Dunc without even haggling. The little shit beams with joy, quickly counting his cash at lightning speed.

"It's all there, young man. Good to do business with you. You've made the right choice today."

I sense he knows the record has a message for me, but he gives nothing away.

Now the market buzzes with music and laughter that travels all the way along the riverfront. The fresh smells of all the lush food from the stalls make me hungry.

"Drinks?"

"I'm game, uncle. Make sure I don't forget my record."

"Of course, you've just been rinsed for two grand. He's had you over a barrel there, son. Looks like the drinks are on me."

The sky is clear with the occasional cloud, and a pleasant breeze keeps us cool. We just chill at a popup bar and sink freezing rums like visiting sailors.

I feel a weight off my shoulders, sipping the day away.

The Crow is always brilliant company, and he just makes you feel at ease in his presence. He's always cool, so everyone around him is cool and falls under his spell.

I feel like I should spill the beans about the video and the record, but something was telling me this was a test, and I should remain silent.

❖

CHAPTER 5

WE decide to head up the river to The Crows' favourite little quaint bar, The Tyne, where everybody knows your name.

We quickly head north out of the market and it's rife with SAF guards, a bit too many for my liking.

The Crow turns to me, whispering over his right shoulder,

"Just play it cool, son. I'll get my driver. It's time to vanish."

Every SAF Guard is dressed in tactical SWAT gear with a three-quarter straight sword, truncheon, Taser, and cold hard eyes that peer from out of their military masks.

A deafening microphone echoes out across the market with a sharp, mean voice. "Mass gatherings are now prohibited after 8 p.m. The market is now closed, disperse at once in an orderly fashion."

My stomach started to churn, and I could feel something was wrong in my gut.

Suddenly, the sound of a swarm of bees fills the air as drones' whizz through the market, taking footage of everyone.

The spies in the sky are great at putting people on edge.

A large military meat van skids to a stop and swings open its rear doors. The guards burst out, and you can feel the tension in the air. They begin to exchange heated words with people, becoming increasingly heavy-handed with the crowds, trying to clear the market and force people to leave.

It's only a matter of time before someone threw the first punch. The locals won't be pushed around like this. With a sudden explosive movement, one of the guards nearly cracks open the head of an old man walking too slowly, as bystanders watch in horror.

A fight breaks out, and the guards seem to change their tactics. They start dragging innocent passersby to the centre of the market; they're cable-tied and thrown face down onto the concrete, ready to be loaded into the van. For what?

I spin to my uncle.

"We have to do something."

"We're in the wrong place at the wrong time, and this is not our fight," he says firmly.

We dart through the crowd, weaving through the sea of strangers. Glancing over my right shoulder, the guards are hot on our heels. The Crow pulls out his phone from his inside pocket and screams to his driver, "Step on it, Dean, we need to get out of here! It's come on top, pick us up at the very end of the market at the record stall."

We're moving swiftly now, getting away from the guards without drawing attention to ourselves.

Dunc grabs us and pulls us into his stall.

"Keep your heads down, lads, it's not worth getting nicked from these bastards."

Looking through the market, I hear booming in the distance. The deafening sound travels up my legs and into my chest. The thunderous noise gets louder and louder, and the force knocks stall after stall over in the distance. I turn to The Crow, concerned, as The SAF cavalry suddenly bursts through the market and their commander screams,

"Charge!"

The cavalry lay down heavy blows, cracking heads of bystanders below them, circling the crowds, angrily lunging with their truncheons.

It knocks me sick at the liberty they're taking.

"Let's bail, Jim," says The Crow.

We quickly make our escape at the back of Dunc's stall; The Crow's driver, Dean, must be waiting for us, I think nervously.

The sound of heavy steps approaches us from behind, and at least fifteen SAF guards circle us. My eyes dart from one side to the other. There's no escape as they form a tight circle around us.

This situation doesn't seem to bother The Crow one bit. I, on the other hand, am experiencing my first bout of claustrophobia.

"Where do you think you're going, hotshot?" the leader hisses.

I reply quickly, rubbing the sweat from my forehead,

"We don't want any trouble. We're just going home."

The guard sniggers, "You're going in the back of the van. That's the only place you're going."

The Crow replies in a stern, assertive voice,

"You've made a grave mistake stopping us. Let us go through and you won't be harmed."

The guards let out a roar of laughter, and then they all snap open their telescopic batons at the same time in synchronized military fashion.

We are royally screwed—fifteen-to-two are canny odds.

The Crow steps closer to the guard who is clearly the commander, blazes on his cigar, and the rich aroma fills the air as he exhales a thick cloud of smoke into the guard's face. He then proceeds to flick the butt of his cigar at his sidekick's head. Everyone pauses in shock, me included, it was like time had stood still.

He unbuttons his long mac and steps back slowly, directly into the centre of the circle of guards. He vibrates the words loudly so everyone can hear. "YOD-HEH-VAU-HEH! YOD-HEH-VAU-HEH!"

The commander looks puzzled. It sounds like some ancient Hebrew language to me.

The sun sparkles on the commander's releasing sword blade.

Baring his teeth in a vicious rant, the cold look in his eyes is filled with raw anger. "Let's just slit their throats." He snarls. "I don't like my time wasted by buffoons."

The Crow opens his mac, arms stretched out as though he's about to take flight from the circle, lifting his hands in an eagle-type soar and crashing them down, screaming the words,

"YOD-HEH-VAU-HEH!"

An electric blue flame pentagram bursts from his mac, letting out a sonic boom of thunderous force, instantly knocking all the surrounding guards to their feet.

There's a huge splash, and some of them fall into the river below, screaming for help as their heavy body armour drags them to their deaths under the current. I look up at my uncle's face. His eyes are wide with anger.

The new crowd that has gathered at our end of the market cheers, and I get the sense this is a nod for us to fight back.

The Crow shouts in a voice I've never heard before, vibrating through the market.

"Magicians, reveal yourselves!"

I can't believe what I'm witnessing.

Approaching, mounted horses pick up speed, guards galloping toward us. They look like they're flying as they travel at a vast speed.

The Crow spins on the spot with his arms out of his mac, creating a soaring circular wind, building up and up like a mini tornado around him.

He starts screaming that strange language again.

"YOD-HEH-VAU-HEH! ADONAI! EHEIEH! AGLA!"

I dive to my uncle's side as he punches his arms to the floor, releasing the tornado. The horses screech, rearing on their back legs, throwing the guards violently from their saddles onto the concrete and hurling some of them into the river.

I was too busy watching The Crow in awe and didn't notice the guard sprinting towards me until too late; he kicked me so hard in the balls it made the strangest noise.

It sounded like a dessert trifle hitting a tiled kitchen floor and the type of pain I would never forget.

He tries to strike me again. Each blow whizzes past me, left to right. I give him credit for the cheap shot, but it's time to knock this fool out.

I hit him with an almighty Byker tea cake. The first rule of head-butting someone is to make sure they're not wearing a tactical solid helmet.

I skid back a few steps and lunge forward with a rear front kick direct to his jaw. He flies back with a deafening crash. The boxes crumple and buckle under his weight as he skids across the concrete floor. The impact has finished his lifeless body off for sure.

Dunc appears with an arm full of records.

"It's time for some banishing!" he shouts, his voice trembling with pure rage.

The records whizz past like mini grinders as the guard's scramble for cover. He frisbees them away rapidly in machine gun fashion, chopping them down with deadly precision. The records continue to rain down on them, and there's nowhere to hide. Through the haze of smoke and dust, Dunc has manifested a horrific scene. The guards are diced up in a bloodbath.

As he chops down the last of them, I realise I've found my Coven.

The magicians were hidden in plain sight the whole time.

❖

CHAPTER 6

IN the distance, the SAFs' reinforcements roar up the River Tyne towards the market.

I knew it wouldn't take them long to mobilise more backup.

Gunboats jump in the air, leaving wave after wave behind either side of a monstrous black and grey camouflage hovercraft that looms over The Quayside. It glides over the water with such might, propelling the enemy forward. It's colossal shadow has me hypnotised as I nearly fall into the river.

Mini battle drones fly above them, approaching like a pack of angry seagulls, suddenly releasing their spinning Gatling guns, emptying round after round into the far end of the market.

Blazing fires suddenly ignite everywhere. The spinning guns cut down innocents and rising magicians.

Amora and Crowley look insane with anger as they approach, thick and fast, on their powerful hovercraft.

Her glare intensifies, and her eyes lock on mine in the distance as she drags her thumb across her throat. Now I don't know sign language, but I'm sure that's the universal sign that she's going to slit my throat.

The ice queen is showing her true colours now.

My uncle quickly covers us with his magical mac, as the hovercraft roars past us.

"Don't worry son, we are invisible while under here."

We quickly bolt through the rear of the market now that the coast is clear.

Glancing back, the stalls are shattered and now lie engulfed in ferocious flames, dark, claustrophobic smoke filling the air. The intense heat causes me to edge backward, away from the attack.

With total disregard for his own life, Duncan runs back into the carnage, spinning sparking records at his fingertips. We leave a fierce battle raging on.

My eyes lock onto two Mercedes S-Class vehicles with blacked-out windows, standing waiting in the billowing smoke.

Thank God - it's The Crow's bodyguards.

We're quickly ushered into the back of the first car by a serious-looking six-foot killer, holding onto his automatic weapon hidden inside his black suit.

We speed off in a double car convoy across the city, the rear car driving bumper to bumper with us as a crash car, ready to run anything off the road so we can escape to safety. The cars skid to an angry stop at the rear of Oyster Soul. Uncle Crow barks at his men, "The restaurant is closed. Guard the front door and don't let anybody through."

We head through a side door that parts to gleaming, illuminated workstations from the deserted kitchen. The Crow seems upbeat and shouts, "We aren't dead yet, so let's have a good time."

He rummages through the leftover plates in the American-style fridge, bursts through the cowboy saloon doors and leads us into the main bar area with fresh lobster and the best vino money can buy.

"What the hell happened out there, Uncle?" I ask as the adrenaline leaves my body.

"It's been a long time coming despite the massacre. Perhaps it's a good thing that magicians are on the rise. We can't just sit back and let the whole country be swallowed up by the SAF."

"They are like a virus that could spread over the entire world. General Saturn is a true psychopath with an uncontrollable lust for violence. His torture campaign on the rise to the top has cost too many innocent lives. They have covered London with missing persons posters, but everyone just ignores it."

He chugs away at his wine. I just sit silently and let him get everything off his chest.

"After his victory speech today, how could he drum up support for such a byzantine corporation?"

He finally states, "The North will not fall into his hands, I assure you."

"How come you've hidden this from me, my whole life, Uncle?"

He pauses for a second.

"Your dad should have told you years ago about our family and the importance of The Gunner bloodline. We have a long history of magic and sworn oaths."

My head is spinning now.

"Hold on, Uncle. I thought we were just a successful family business?"

He shakes his head as though I should have known something was up.

"Follow the dots, Jim. How do you think we're so successful? We use secret wealth magic in all our endeavour's. All will be revealed to you, in good time, on your path to illumination." He's talking in riddles again, infuriating me.

Our conversation is cut off as Uncle Crow falls silent and peers through the blinds of the bar window. Gunboats are on full alert now as they soar up and down the River Tyne.

He turns to his bodyguard. "We'll hide out here until things calm down. Make sure you organize backup. This is heavy work, so get our best men. We'll be leaving at dawn." His menacing bodyguard just nods and marches off.

The Crow seems unaffected by the last couple of hours. After what we've just gone through, my hands are still trembling. I've never seen carnage like it.

He approaches his favourite vintage jukebox. The warm glow of the neon lights illuminates his happy face. Spinning with a wide grin, *The Killing Moon* by Echo and the Bunnymen booms through the bar, and he slams a bottle of honey Jack Daniels onto the table with a bucket of ice.

"Let's toast to the Gunner family," he says, pouring us each a heavy measure.

"Did you have an accident out there, Jim?" he asks with a smirk on his face.

"How do you mean?"

"I mean, did you shit yourself? I've got some spare clothes and a shower out the back if you need to get cleaned up," laughing hysterically.

"Piss off, I'm fine. I've never witnessed anything like that before."

"I see you've still got your record from Dunc in your jacket."

"I wasn't losing that, plus there was a message for me on the sleeve." I say, holding it closely to my chest.

He leans in with a puzzled face, a mix of curiosity.

"Spill the beans then, who from?"

"The Coven. It says that I must get to Holy Island pier by 7 p.m. tomorrow."

"You know what this means? You've been called upon; it's your time to prove yourself and make the Gunners proud. It is of paramount importance that we get you to Holy Island in one piece and you do not deviate from the Coven's request."

It's an enormous leap of faith to think I can stand up to the SAF by myself, I think to myself.

"What will you do, Uncle, if I go?"

"While I'm not nervous about the ramifications of the SAF today, I'll do what I do best - disappear off the face of the earth."

He dances over to the jukebox again with all his favourite songs and *Leaving on a Jet Plane* by John Denver echoes through the bar. He's singing and spinning around in a happy drunken haze.

He heads back over to the main window again, making me nervous.

"The coast is clear, bonny lad. I'll have my driver take you to Holy Island in the morning."

Feeling a vibration in my top pocket, I reach for my phone.

There's a security alert. Someone is outside my apartment's front door.

We both peer nervously at the large screen. We hear a huge banging, and then suddenly, SAF guards flatten the front door and burst into my apartment. Nipper runs at them with no fear.

"Don't you dare!" I scream. One of the evil bastards shoots him with a Taser.

Nipper falls in a heap, skidding along the wooden floor.

He had better be ok.

I will not rest until I put that man into the ground.

We watch as the guards turn my apartment upside down, ripping, smashing and destroying everything I've worked hard for. One goon points up at the camera in the entrance.

Amora cruises through the door and pulls the camera towards her face, staring into it with dead eyes.

"We will find you, James, and when we do, your family and everyone you know will suffer."

The camera cuts off on the phone into white noise, leaving a sinister exit from the bitch.

I snatch the whiskey bottle and start glugging away.

The Crow knocks it out of my hand, smashing it across the floor, leaving shards of glass everywhere.

"You've had enough to drink," he snaps. "You need to be on the ball for tomorrow, so there are no mistakes."

"Sorry uncle, I'm just upset."

"Nipper will be fine. It will take more than a few volts to put him down."

The fun has vanished from his eyes. Passing me a blanket, he says,

"Get your head down, you need your rest. I'll clean the mess up tomorrow."

I drift into a deep sleep, the exhaustion of today's events hitting me.

It feels like five minutes later when The Crow clicks his fingers loudly in my face. "Wake up, Jim, your driver is outside," he growls.

Rubbing my eyes, I drag myself into an upright position. I look at an antique wall clock that says it's 5:15 a.m. "Come on, there's no time for games. Get up, we've made the news."

I wouldn't be surprised if he's been up the whole night, curtain twitching with anticipation.

"What did the news say?" I reply.

"They're looking for us and a record dealer known as Duncan, involved in a serious incident at the market."

"That's it?"

"Well, they're not going to go into details about me dismantling their entire force. There's a fifty grand reward on us."

"No way." I can't believe there's a reward on our heads.

"Every shit house in Newcastle will crawl out from underneath their rocks to hand us in," Uncle Crow snarls.

"What are you going to do?"

"Disappear. I've got safe houses up in Scotland."

I like The Crow's confidence and it's obvious he's been in sticky situations like this before.

We exit from the rear of the restaurant, leaving the way we came in. I can see the SAF boats lying silently tied up along the river.

All I can hear are birds singing. There isn't a soul around, and it's perfect timing for our escape.

A solidly built man who looks hard as nails stands next to the Mercedes saloon. He looks like he's done a lot of jail time. He wears it on his face.

The Crow introduces us,

"This is Robert, my best driver and bodyguard." He nods – another of my uncles' men with few words and no time for small talk.

The Crow releases the automatic boot of the saloon.

"Get in, James."

"Really, Uncle?"

He steps in closer and puts his arm around me,

"Make us proud, James."

Luckily, I just fit as I'm sandwiched into the boot.

The last thing I see is my uncle's smiling face as Robert slams the boot down. It's pitch black but comfortable. The sound of the engine roars and we take off at high speed, winding through hills and heading north.

Robert is double paranoid in case we are being followed, and what should be an hour and a half journey turns into a full-day event. We switch cars twice, stopping off at various safe houses throughout Northumberland and stuffing me back into the boot of each car. The gentle hum of the engine and each turn and curve rock me to sleep.

I wake up in fright.

The terrain is much rougher, and I can hear water gushing under the wheels. I'm knocked back and forth for a good fifteen minutes. The sound of the water concerns me.

I start to punch the side of the boot and scream Robert's name over and over. I can't think of anything worse than drowning in this little rocking coffin.

We skid to a sudden stop, and I hear loud footsteps, then a blinding bright light blasts into the boot. Squinting, I shout,

"What the hell, Robert? I thought I was going to drown."

He just drags me out of the boot with one hand, using his immense strength.

"I'm going to have to ditch you here, or I'll get stranded going back with the high tide, and I'd be the one drowning."

I look left to right, and we've reached the end of the dramatic causeway of Holy Island.

I've got a couple of miles before I reach the rendezvous point. I'd rather navigate through the marsh and dunes in the last of the daylight, so I'd better start moving.

"Your uncle rang earlier and said Newcastle is on full lockdown. They have flooded the entire city with SAF special forces troops." I shake my head in disbelief.

"I don't understand – all of this for me and my uncle?"

"They're hiding it in the news, saying it's a suspected terrorist attack, giving them the green light for their heavy presence in the city."

They are clearly using us as a scapegoat for their tightening grip on the north. I hold my hands against the back of my head and deeply inhale the clean sea air. Robert points along the dunes of the wild coast.

"You want to be two miles east of here." He shakes my hand with his iron grip, "Godspeed, James."

He wheels away, leaving gravel and dust at my feet. I begin with a light jog, flashing my watch up. It's 6:20 p.m., so I pick up the pace, now getting into a steady rhythm. My mind turns over and over with worry. I hope my uncle has escaped, and I wonder what has become of Duncan. The last time I saw him; he vanished into a hail of smoke.

I reach the pretty little town of Holy Island, lightly jogging past some small stone cottages as they stand timeless, full of rustic charm, and I'm right on time. Gazing up at the sky, the rainbow stone arch is a sight to see in the Lindisfarne Priory ruins. I can see why the monks lived here. The island is so peaceful it's hard to imagine the brutal attacks of the raiding Vikings that decimated the place hundreds of years ago.

❖

CHAPTER 7

THE historical remains cast a spell on me as I look left to right across the priory. It's as though time has stood still, and it's 7 p.m. on the dot. I can't see anybody - just a fleet of old wooden boats turned upside down, running along the side of the stone pier.

One of those would be perfect to sleep under if my contact from the The Coven chooses not to reveal themselves.

There is a silhouette in one alcove of the ruins. A tall, frail, smartly dressed man in a black vintage suede suit and black polka dot silk scarf that dances lightly in the summer wind approaching.

With a long, well-kept silver beard and a dramatic antique wooden cane that looks priceless.

I'd recognise those sinking ice-blue eyes anywhere.

I sprint towards him, picking him up and spin him around.

"Grandad, I thought you were gone for good," I say as I squeeze him tightly.

"James, you're hurting me. Put me down."

Our laughter echoes across the ruins, filling the air with joy, and we connect instantly as though I only saw him yesterday.

"Come quickly," he whispers into my left ear. "Let us walk through the ruins of the priory and away from prying eyes."

It's deadly quiet; you can hear the waves in the distance lapping up on the shore. Taking a seat on a huge old sandstone rock that could be a gravestone, it's too hard to make out as time hasn't been kind to the crumbling rock.

I look across the bay to the left, and Lindisfarne Castle stands proudly on its rock. To the right, across the beautiful Northumberland coastline, the mighty Bamburgh Castle stands guard in the distance.

"You should have reached out to me, so I knew you were OK, Grandad."

"I couldn't, son. It would have brought too much attention to my attempted assassination."

"What do you mean, attention?" I ask.

"There were too many witnesses on Main Street at the time. I should have been chopped in half with the hail of bullets. They fired enough from their machine guns to bring down an African elephant. There wasn't a scratch on me, so I had to disappear. The Youngs probably thought they'd done a number on me."

"How did you not get hurt?"

With a stern voice, he replies, "Through our magical lineage. My subconscious mind instantly turns my aura into a solid shield, deflecting every bullet. I escaped to my safe house in the mountains of Scotland."

"My dad said you would hide in the mountains. I thought he was taking the piss."

He looks at me with sad eyes. "It's a bitter pill to swallow, and time moves so slowly up there. I'm sorry, James, my intention was never to hurt anyone, but I had to protect the Gunner family name. I knew one day you would awaken to your higher consciousness."

My head spins now with all this new information, but I want to know more.

"What do you mean, higher consciousness?"

He turns to me with a broad smile that brings colour back into his cheeks. "To know, to dare, to will, to keep silent," he says in a smooth voice.

He's talking in riddles.

"Now tell me, James, what have you been feeling?"

"To be honest, my head has been in bits. I've been feeling like the world is spinning the wrong way most days, and I can't relate to anyone or anything in my life. Then I see numbers everywhere."

He chuckles. "What numbers have you seen?"

"It all started with eleven/eleven."

He thumps his cane once on the floor of the ruin below.

"Ah, the pillars on either side of you," he sighs. "And then?"

"Twenty-two/twenty-two."

"The transformation," he shouts with a double thump of the cane, looking at me directly in my eyes with anticipation.

"Then all I see is thirty-three or three threes everywhere," I continue.

He triple, thumps his cane, and jumps up.

"The great awakening to your higher self," he says loudly and proudly. To be honest, I've never seen him look so proud.

"What does this all mean, though?"

He is quiet for a moment or two, looking out onto the beautiful coast as though he is gaining knowledge from the horizon. He deeply inhales the clear sea air and whispers,

"The Gunner family is part of a sacred order to protect

The Seal of 33. We are here to protect the very fabric of the universe and everything that vibrates in its existence."

Grandad continues as the darkness of night closes in.

"The SAF are on the rise, and this is the reason The Seal has to be protected." I had a feeling this is all about them.

"Their goal is for the one mind to be switched off and for humanity to fall into a deep sleep."

The pieces of this puzzle finally come together; I think. It's nice to have some solid answers to what is going on in the world right now.

"They are doing everything in their power to end consciousness and true free will. Nobody took them seriously at first, but with General Saturn's unlimited wealth and resources, London was the first to fall easily. They now call it Stone City. Most people have had the upgrade chip, and it's only populated by Greys."

I can feel something is truly wrong in the pit of my stomach. "What are the Greys?"

"They've sold their soul son, and not to the devil, but to artificial intelligence - something far worse. I may have a vast knowledge of how the world works, but you have time on your side, your greatest asset."

"What can I do to help, Grandad?"

"Every generation gets their turn, and today is the day you leave to train for war. History seems to repeat itself, and soon, the world will fall into chaos. The Coven has called on you to be a protector of The Seal."

He points to his beautiful handcrafted wooden vine cane, lifting the ball at the top and revealing a hidden gold-red ruby ring.

"Take this, James. It's been in the family since the dawn of time."

The ring has a perfectly set ruby resting in the centre,

with two lions' heads on either side.

I slide the ring onto my right little finger, and my feet are firmly planted to the ground. It's as if the ground beneath me has come alive, and I'm connected to the mystical universal forces.

"This is the Talisman ring. Only use it as your last option when all else fails and you are in grave danger, as you can only summon its power once."

I'm a bit baffled but try not to show it.

"How do I call on its power?"

A big thump from his cane again makes me stand to attention.

"Spin the Talisman around the ruby clockwise all the way round, then fully anticlockwise, then press the ruby and instantly vibrate the words. I call on thee. RAH-ZEE-ELL, the gatekeeper of the universe. Come forth and protect me."

This is a lot to remember; I feel I should be taking notes.

"What happens now then, Grandad?"

"Be vigilant, keep your head up and your heart strong. It's time to make our move now."

He leads the way, and I quickly follow his footsteps to the right, weaving through the ruins until we arrive at the start of a short stone pier that overlooks the peaceful sea.

A handful of battered local fishing boats are tied up and moored at the muddy harbour. We head past them, right to the end of the pier.

"The Coven has organised a meeting from here. This is your initiation into the sacred order. They will reveal everything to you in good time."

All I can make out in the darkness are yachts and pleasure boats anchored around me.

Grandad raises his right hand with his wooden cane high into the night sky. The boat's light flickers to life, and a powerful beam of light crosses the water, lighting up the whole harbour. The mighty boat's engine roars to life as its unstoppable force cuts through the water toward us. I can just make out the name on the boat's side, Odyssey, painted in deep red.

"This is your safe passage to Malta. Captain Sid is the best man for the job, and he will get you there in one piece."

The captain pulls alongside us, throwing me a line as the strong stench of petrol burns my nostrils.

"Tie it off, young man," he shouts.

I didn't have a clue what I was doing but jumped into action, swiftly looping the line around an old, splintered post. I gift wrapped the post enough times, anchoring the boat to the safety of the harbour.

He's a short, strong looking man with a twiddly thick moustache and a young-looking face. He has old sailor tattoos dotted up both powerful arms, wrapped in anchors and mermaids that haven't aged well at all.

He jumps onto the pier, runs and picks up my Grandad with a bear hug.

"You old bugger, how the devil are you? It must be fifteen years since I've seen you!" he shouts, without pausing for breath. "I have an important request to deliver a Mr. James Gunner to the harbour of Valletta. What's this job then, old man?"

He crushes my right hand and pulls me to an inviting embrace, whispering in my right ear. "I take it that's you, young man?"

Without giving me a chance to respond, "OK, lets get this show on the road," he shouts. Eagerly tossing the line back onto the boat, leaving no time for small talk.

I hug my grandad again and tell him I love him. I feel a surge of emotion welling up from the tips of my toes to the top of my head. Tears fill my eyes, and I struggle to contain the rush of feelings. I quickly leap onto the fishing boat before any waterworks start.

Captain Sid takes the large wooden wheel and starts up the motor of the boat, the smell of petrol once again invading the air. We set sail as I look back at the pier and wonder if I will ever see my grandad again, waving to him until he becomes a small dot.

We soar ahead as the engine picks up speed, leaving wave after wave behind.

I pull myself along the razor-sharp fishing nets hanging at the side of the boat, nearly dicing my hands to bits on the sharp edges. The smell of fish guts is unbearable, entwined with petrol fumes, knocking me sick.

Captain Sid is an upbeat jolly fellow.

"Don't worry," he shouts over the engines, "I'll get you to Malta. I've been in this game since I was knee high." Towering black clouds roll over in front of us, making our escape that bit harder to navigate. The sound of the sea is mesmerising as we chug along in the dark, with only the moon in the sky to keep us on course.

Captain Sid grips the wheel and gives his command.

"You'd best get below deck, James. There's a storm coming. There's warm food if you're hungry, just keep out of sight until we get through any checkpoints, and I'll wake you if need be."

"OK," I shout over the sound of the engine.

I clearly haven't developed my sea legs yet, as I skid down the wooden flight of stairs and smash my head on the low wooden joist with a spine-crunching thump. The smell of the fish guts is still hijacking my nostrils, and its bastard freezing down here.

I grab a heavy knitted orange jumper, fit for Freddy

Krueger, pulling it over my head as I head through the galley, banging each shoulder, rocking through the boat.

I feel sorry for the captain as violent waves rage from the unforgiving North Sea. Feeling a tad seasick already, I quickly clamber into a bunk, getting bashed from side to side. I close my eyes tightly and make a wish.

"Please get us to Malta safely," I whisper.

❖

CHAPTER 8

THE world around me emerges in a hazy blur. It's a running joke in my family that I can fall asleep anywhere. The boat rocked me like a baby, straight to sleep.

I rub my eyes and jump off the bunk with a groaning stomach. I eagerly follow the captivating smell of homemade chicken soup, heading through the cozy little galley and squeezing myself into a chair at the square wooden table.

Feeling ravenous, I dive into the pan of soup sitting at the centre of the table and tear the tiger bread loaf to pieces that's placed next to it, using it as a makeshift spoon. Eating like a gentleman goes out the window down here.

Deafening foghorns suddenly blast out all around me. I quickly jump up and dart through the galley but can't see anything outside the port side windows. They're way too small. I have the sinking feeling that these lights are from SAF patrol boats.

As loud as the sea, a voice crackles over the microphone,

"Stop your fishing boat now, you are out of the boundaries." My heart pounds. It is The SAF.

The captain slows The Odyssey down to a chugging stop.

With a stern voice, another order barks, "You have thirty seconds to turn around or we will open fire and destroy your vessel."

Captain Sid obeys their demands. Am I going to be executed on the spot? I race up the slippery wooden steps onto the freezing deck.

"Get up here!" he screams, "Take the wheel, but keep out of sight."

Taking hold of the large wooden wheel, I keep the boat steady.

"When I shout go, push the throttle fully forward," Captain Sid says, pointing at the lever.

He sounds like he has a getaway plan—I hope so.

The SAF's lights and sirens light up the sky now. Captain Sid approaches the stern with his arms held high to make sure he's not shot. The angry-looking sailors have their guns fixated on him.

"I'm really sorry, boys, the storm's got the better of me and knocked me off course."

The microphone crackles back on. "Follow us in now, and you won't be prosecuted."

"OK, skipper!" he shouts out with a thumbs-up, held high.

The SAF gunboats turn around, leading us to follow them back to shore.

"Go, Jim!" he screams.

I jump to his command, cranking the throttle forward and spinning the wheel fully to a hard right. The engine roars, and the bow violently lifts. Captain Sid jumps to safety, clinging onto some fishing nets just before he gets thrown overboard.

Holding onto the wheel for dear life, I use all my strength to keep it on course.

Looking over my right shoulder, lights and sirens chase us, following us into the dead of the night. Mayhem suddenly erupts around us, and rocket propelled grenades scream through the sky. They land on either side of the boat. Powerful waves crash against the deck. The thunderous impact knocks me straight to the floor, helpless. I raise my right arm and manage to grab the old wooden wheel. The next grenades won't miss, I think. I'm absolutely drenched.

Smaller gunboats catch up to us and unleash their Gatling gun fury. Bullets splinter up the deck and chase the soles of the captain's feet. He dives into the helm, taking cover.

The SAF is vastly gaining on us in speed and in numbers, bouncing on every wave behind. The next barrage of gunfire will surely sink us.

The Captain snipes along the deck to the wheel and jumps up. As his hands take control of the wheel, I notice he's wearing a similar ring to my Talisman ring.

He spins the dial on his ring North to South then back to North and presses the green stone in the centre, shouting,

"I call on thee, Poseidon of the sea, open a portal for us to flee."

I can't believe my eyes. A further hail of machine-gun bullets whizz past our heads. Their relentless pursuit drives us to the brink of desperation. A dazzling portal crackles and sparkles, ten meters in front of us. Golden rays of sunlight burst through a growing hole that opens at a rapid pace.

The captain screams with joy, "It's our gateway."

We are swiftly swallowed up by the shimmering portal.

In the blink of an eye, we are plunged into a new world. We are transported from thunderous, dark, life-threatening skies to a calm and bright azure horizon.

❖

CHAPTER 9

THE boat's stern creaks and shakes. Water starts to pour in over the sides, slowly swallowing the rear. We've taken too much gunfire, and we are creeping along; thank God we are only ten minutes from Malta's port. The captain seemed strangely upbeat in this crisis.

"Don't fret, James, The Odyssey will get us to shore."

If the boat was in good shape, we could have just sailed into the sunset and forgotten all about The Coven's proposal. An easier life, maybe.

He spins the wheel through his hands like a true sailor, making a hard left. I look on in awe at the ancient city of Valletta's monstrous walls.

We chug through the port gates and calamity strikes again as we crudely crash into the dock. The sound of the impact echoes through surrounding buildings and onlookers gasp in horror.

The captain looks relieved, wiping heavy sweat from his brow.

"She's done, Jim. She's done me proud with the voyages we've been on."

The boat is a total wreck, with hundreds of bullet holes splintering every piece of wood you can see. I feel gutted.

The Odyssey is on the brink of sinking. All of this just to get me to safety.

I turn and shake my head.

"I'm so sorry about your boat, Captain."

"Don't worry, Jim. The Coven will foot the repair. It's not like it hasn't happened before."

The captain passes me a small sealed white envelope with a red wax letter "C" on the front, a wide grin on his face, and an iron handshake.

"I bid you farewell and all the luck in the world, but it's time for you to take off."

The only exit I can see is a short walk along the marina. I spin and thank the captain, marching off. I carefully break the seal as my eyes scan the words. It says, in beautiful gold calligraphy, *Queen Victoria Statue, Republic Square, 8 p.m.* It's not much information to go by.

I pass an old homeless man with a leather face that's seen too much sun. He's sitting, feeding the birds on the floor. I ask him for directions to the square. He flashes me a smile of broken teeth and points up to a never-ending flight of stone steps.

It must be over 38 degrees Celsius. My thighs burn as I scale the never-ending flight of stairs. My breathing becomes heavy, as I wasn't used to running in such blistering heat. I reach the top, ready to jump like Rocky Balboa. I catch my breath and regain my focus. A cobblestone street path leads me around a corner onto Republic Square.

The square is enclosed on three sides by an impressive limestone building, the main feature being the entrance to The National Library. Trees line each side, leading up to the impressive façade dominating the square, oozing with history.

The crowds are packed between the trees lining the

square, squeezed onto the café tables and chairs.

I put on my shades and take a seat at the base of a stern statue of Queen Victoria. I'm glad I'm sitting away from all the holidaymakers and the pigeons scavenging for scraps. I order a cappuccino from a friendly waiter and look around for my contact.

The square is a beautiful sight to behold. Laughter fills the air from locals and holidaymakers as they sip coffee and chat eagerly with each other, hours passing by. It's nice and peaceful, but there is no sign of my contact, and it's beginning to concern me.

Now it is way after 8 p.m., and the sun begins to set behind the beautiful buildings that house the historic library. The clatter of the cutlery fills the square as the waiters tidy up the tables and people disperse into the night. Another good hour passes before the square falls deadly silent. I probably look odd, as I'm the only one seated.

"You, boy," I quickly look left and to my right, but nobody is in sight. "Up here, you fool."

I think it's a product of my imagination. I shake my head, squeeze my eyes tightly, and release them.

I can't believe it. The Queen Victoria statue is addressing me.

Suddenly, the statue seems to take a deep breath, and with a gentle rustle of fabric, Queen Victoria steps down from her pedestal. She surveys her surroundings with true regal grace.

"Do you not normally kneel in the presence of a queen?"

I quickly kneel, feeling the cold ground on my right knee, and look up into the statue's face.

She's wearing a detailed lace shawl, scepter, and a book in her left hand.

She suddenly becomes deadly still, except for strangely human-like eyes and lips, which are moving as she barks at me.

"You look pathetic. Get up, boy." She laughs hysterically. "Come closer. I have a message for you: proceed to the Lower Barrakka Gardens by dawn tomorrow. You will find what you're looking for."

"Surely you have more to tell me." I'm frantic now. I'm stuck on a strange island talking to a statue. "Please, tell me." I grapple with the mystery of another secret message.

A voice to my left interrupts. "Excuse me, who are you talking to?"

I must look insane to the waiter cleaning up.

"Nobody," I grumble.

The queen's face has turned back to stone in the blink of an eye.

I quickly walk off into the moonlight and travel along more cobblestone paths. Heading through another grand archway, there's not a soul in sight.

I proceed down some winding stairs. It was pitch black now.

A wooden sign points toward the Lower Barrakka Gardens, marking the entrance to a beautiful ancient structure that looks like it holds real historical significance.

I enter the temple grounds, soaking up its peaceful, silent gardens, and find an ancient, weathered stone bench in the corner beneath an old, wise oak tree that's out of sight. Its large branches stretch out like comforting arms. There's nothing I can do but take shelter here.

The last thing I remember is an owl calling out, and I must have fallen into a deep sleep from pure exhaustion.

The sun rises, breaking through the trees of the gardens. I feel at peace for the first time in days as the rays warm my skin, and I take in the beauty of the gardens surrounding me.

A tall, strong-looking man with dark skin and a silver beard appears suddenly from behind a tree, startling me. He wears a beige robe wrapped tightly around him with his hood up.

I jump up, brushing myself down, and think, please be my contact and not some creep lurking in the gardens. I peer into the darkness of his hood but can't make out his face.

His voice echoes, "Are you Mr. James Gunner?"

"I am," I reply.

How could this stranger know me?

"Who are you?"

"They call me The Great Architect, your contact from The Coven."

I can feel the anger boiling up inside me.

"Some contact you are," I shout. "I've been chased from the North of England through portals, to stone statues giving me messages and I've been sleeping outside like a wild animal."

He reaches up and pulls the hood of his beige cloak down, revealing a friendly face with sparkling emerald, green eyes.

Hypnotising me with his bright smile, he speaks in a quiet, reassuring voice, "Welcome to the Mystery School of Malta. I'll be your teacher and guide through the great work. We have limited time for you to master battle magic."

The Architect's face never changes as he explains the very fate of the universe to me. He has a smooth way of talking as his voice softens a bit, revealing more of The Coven's plan.

"The world is falling into the wrong hands. The

Shadow Advanced Federation and General Saturn will do everything in their power to turn off the one mind and cause humanity to fall into a deep sleep."

I listen intently now, as he doesn't mince his words. "What is magic?"

"It's the ancient powers that have been lost through time. They built the great Egyptian pyramids using this power. Every human being is equal. You all have the divine spark, and the human spirit is capable of anything. At the beginning of your magical path, there will be doubts, challenges, obstacles, and mistakes. All of this is normal through the great work. Let us walk."

We stroll through the gardens in silence for a few minutes, taking in the scenery and sounds of birds, singing their morning song. The air is filled with the sweet perfume of vibrant flowers.

The Architect stops abruptly and clicks his right fingers.

A beautiful faint orange glow ignites from his index finger, drawing a large circle of mysterious energy in front of him, two meters high. It literally burns through the air, like a children's sparkler. I am full of anticipation at what he has up his sleeves.

He spins to face me, looking proud.

"You'll be glad to know that you're not the only one who has been called upon by The Coven. Meet your fellow magicians, Sky Gray and Layla Rose."

Stepping elegantly through the circular portal that he draws are the two most beautiful women I have ever seen. They both wear matching black satin full-length cloaks with their hoods up, and long satin gloves up to the middle of their arms. Black tiny mini dresses and six-inch Louboutin heels.

"Hello, James," they both say in sequence. I smile at them both.

Sky stands to the left. Her dark chocolate-perfect skin and flawless complexion would have me addicted in no time. Layla stands to the right, a beautiful white girl with blonde hair and sparkling blue eyes.

The two are perfect polarities.

I think I'd best introduce myself.

"Hello, I'm James Gunner, your magical companion."

They both let out a sweet laugh. Finally, I am dealt a good hand.

There isn't a cloud in the sky, and the sun is scorching hot now. The Architect pulls his hood back up, and the mood changes as we wait in silence.

"We only have six short weeks to get you proficient in the great work."

Layla asks in a sweet-sounding voice, "Will we be learning white or black magic?"

The Architect laughs, "That depends on your soul, my dear. You will learn to quieten the mind, ground yourself and break away from the lower vibration the masses are trapped in. You will gain composure and inner strength, standing on your own as a middle pillar at the centre of the universe. Then, you will conquer the elements, leading you into great illumination."

I don't know if I should write this down or not. I get the feeling he won't be repeating anything he's saying. At the end of every statement, I give him an assured nod. The girls look like they've been well briefed.

Looks like it's just me starting with a white belt in magic.

The Architect hands me a set of old-fashioned, heavy keys fit for a castle gate and a note with an address.

"I look forward to seeing what the three of you bring to the table on your first day of training."

"The keys are for your townhouse overlooking the grand harbour of Valletta. You won't be disappointed with your lodgings, and please return to the gardens at dawn tomorrow." He says no more and disappears into a line of trees.

We bolt from the gardens after the girls link arms on either side of me. The sun is so hot above us; it feels like it is cracking the pavement.

We skip down the narrow winding streets of Valletta, following the street signs toward the harbour.

The front door of each house is a different vibrant colour, with a matching wooden tiny balcony. They are all unique and full of character. We pass ocean blue, forest green, and wine red, looking at each other with excitement, like children on Christmas morning.

"Here we are!" I shout.

We'll never forget our door.

A hidden gem tucked away in the street's corner. An immaculate canary yellow rustic front door, and a stained-glass dome above, that stands as a grand introduction. I laugh to myself at the number thirty-three painted in black. My lucky number, what a coincidence, and hopefully a good omen. The heavy brass knocker is in the shape of a golden seahorse that sits proudly in the centre. A large, tiled plaque with its name, Coven House, to the right.

I turn the castle key, setting the tone for the treasure that awaits in our new home. The three of us stumble onto an expensive-looking black and white chequered marble floor. A majestic marble spiral staircase leads us up to the first floor with two attractive, chic-looking, minimalistic bedrooms.

"We've got our rooms!" the girls scream with excitement.

I quickly scale the marble stairs to the second floor and am greeted with the master bedroom, an amazing open-plan living space. It is fit for a royal visitor—plush, with a 1930s antique feel, and an enormous, solid-looking four-poster elegantly carved antique bed stands in the centre. Draped with velvet and silk plush quilts and pillows. Large looming mirrors from floor to ceiling stand on either side of the bed.

Cane seats sit in every corner. You could easily get lost reading a good book.

I stride over to the balcony and fling open the handcrafted wooden doors. The blazing sunlight heats the room instantly.

The wide balcony stretches the length of the house, the views of the old exquisite architecture steeped in history take my breath away.

Quaint restaurants and cool bars snake up the harbour with a buzzing atmosphere. I love all the individual, brightly painted fishing boats that rock, cradle-like, for miles to see.

The girls burst into the room and Layla's face looks puzzled.

"James, you have the best room in the house. That's not fair."

"Ah, you shouldn't have jumped in with both feet when you saw the first option. We can swap. I just need a place to sleep," I reply.

She laughs, spinning off onto the balcony to take in the view.

Sky's voice echoes through the building, calling for us to look upstairs.

Wow, our jaws drop. The rooftop terrace offers a breathtaking panoramic view of the harbour. The furniture invites pure relaxation, with large comfortable cushions surrounding the barbecue area. A cool sports bar lounge is stacked high with every drink imaginable. You could sleep up here under the stars, high above the world below.

The girls are true free spirits with matching beautiful smiles. I feel like we have an instant connection.

I think I'll name the rooftop The Wheelhouse.

We get settled into our rooms. With my lucky escape and no clothes with me, I head straight to the wardrobe to see if there is anything I can borrow to wear. I open the double cane doors to reveal many finely tailored suits and casual smart clothing. Everything in the full summer Versace collection is my size. I am buzzing. I fall back in a heap on the four-poster bed, exhausted from all the drama. I'd finally made it to safety.

The sun hits my body, lighting up the whole room. It can't be, but it's 5:30 a.m., the girls are already up and dressed to impress.

"Morning, sorry about last night. I haven't had a good night's sleep for so long, and I think my body just shut down." Layla gives me a warm smile.

"Are you prepared for day one of your journey?" she asks.

"Of course, I'm ready to rock."

The Great Architect appears from behind tall white grand pillars of the prominent monument, standing proudly in the gardens.

"Ah, the magic three," he sighs. "Welcome to day one of The Mystery School. Today, you will learn to quiet the mind and focus on the grid. This is a subtle energy field that is already in your body. Through practice, you will crystallize your aura, and this will harden it and prevent any negative outside forces from manipulating you. When your physical body dies, your aura will be strong enough for you to cross over the veil and break on through to the other side safely and effortlessly."

The Architect tells us to form a circle and sit with our legs crossed tightly, with our spines straight up, so our chakras can gain power.

"OK, follow me."

He continues, "Breathe in for four seconds, hold for four seconds and on the exhale, say the magical word, together. Let the word, together, vibrate in your throat for four seconds. Hold for four seconds, then repeat breathing in through your nostrils deeply."

We all look at each other and shrug our shoulders.

The Architect says, "Close your eyes and let us travel into the abyss. Everything starts in the mind."

We are all lost in the group meditation. Time seems like an illusion.

I'm not even in the gardens anymore. I am gone; I have left this place and fallen into the black nothingness in between worlds.

The girls let out a loud scream, giving me a fright. I open my eyes, and I'm hovering, totally weightless. The force holding me up suddenly disappears, and I crash to the floor in a heap.

"What the hell was that?" Sky screamed. "You were levitating six feet off the floor."

I look at them in disbelief and spin to the Architect, thinking she is winding me up.

"Your levitation demonstration was impeccable." He slowly nods with approval at me.

It's been a long time since I've had any praise. I sense the girls will become overly competitive as I have come out on top today.

The Architect flashes me a wide grin, grooming his immaculate silver beard. His eyes glow like emeralds out of his hood, and he gives me the nod of approval again.

I look down at my watch; we have been in a trance for over four hours.

"Well done, James, you have the power of levitation. Once you've mastered it, you can do it at your will."

I receive a pleasant smile from both girls.

The Architect claps his hands heavily.

"That will be enough for today. You have tomorrow for yourselves. Carry on this practice and return here on Wednesday at 6 a.m. sharp."

Before we even had time to thank him, he had disappeared into thin air, another vanishing act of the highest order.

❖

CHAPTER 10

AN arctic cold shower blasts away the oily sweat from today's practice. I feel a weight lift now, and I'm settled into Coven House. We have arranged to celebrate at The Wheelhouse on the rooftop tonight, and I can smell the fresh fish coming off the terrace. The Coven has provided me with a casual wardrobe. A golden and black Versace Medusa print shirt is wide open after I slip into some beige chino shorts and leather loafers. I look at my reflection in the full-length mirror. My abs are sharp, and my chest is broad. I am looking good and already tanning nicely. I make a pretty good guess, based on the way the stars align in the sky, that I might get lucky with one of the girls tonight. I enter, and both are transfixed, staring at me intensely as I approach The Wheelhouse bar.

"Did someone order tall and handsome!" I shout.

Layla's face lights up, "Check out the Lord of the Manor." Her eyes are so bright as she leans in for a soft kiss. Although brief, it is intense.

They are wearing Indian pink and yellow saris with little or no makeup, both true natural beauties. "You both scrub up well for a couple of witches. Please don't say you're sacrificing a goat for our evening meal."

Sky drums her long red fingernails on top of the bar, handing me an espresso martini. Her pink sari moves so elegantly in the summer breeze, my arm slips around her petite waist, spinning her out and snapping her back into my arms. Our first small kiss is perfection, and there is enough electricity between us to power Malta.

She whispers softly into my right ear, "You sort the tunes out, and I'll fix us some more drinks."

There's an antique record player in the corner of the bar. It's such a beautiful night looking out onto the harbour, mega yachts docked all the way along the pier. The place is buzzing for a Monday night. I dust the vinyl down and place Dion's *Only You Know* onto the turntable. It sets the scene as it blasts across the rooftop. Sky has conjured up a long line of cocktails. We raise our glasses with a sturdy clink of amaretto sours in a toast to the magical three on our new adventure.

We dance the night away, with me twirling both girls out and snapping them back in, extremely close to me. "What did you think of my magic today?" Layla spins away to the dinner table.

"You have some skills, but a lot of your practice is undisciplined. We will see what you bring to the table on Wednesday."

She kisses out hot air from her luscious lips, setting the candles alight in a domino effect the full length of the dinner table.

"Nice trick," I laugh. "You're just showing off now, though."

Dinner is served, and we chat away. Sky is from a powerful family in New York, high on the social scene. Layla is from an insanely rich banking family in London. Both were sent to train in the great work. We play vintage records;

Echo and the Bunnymen's *Nothing Lasts Forever* is spinning. I move on to the next drink – elderflower prosecco with cucumber. I'm quaffing them back in Oliver Reed fashion. I think I've gotten a bit carried away with the excitement.

Layla looks at me with devilry in her eyes.

"So then, Mr. Gunner, how long do you think you'll stay in Valletta for?"

"The way this fairy tale is unravelling, I'll be changing my identity and living up on this rooftop."

The girls are so much fun to be around. I eat my dinner hurriedly, as all I'm interested in are the frozen cocktails and these beauties. More drinks flow. The last thing I remember is falling back onto the sofa, listening to *Mykonos* by Fleet Foxes.

I wake up with a cracking head still on the terrace. The girls must have called it a night and left me up here. The beer fear instantly enters my mind. What a plum. I can't remember anything.

"Morning, Layla."

I skid past her, pinching a piece of her toast.

"Apologies for last night, I think you might have slipped something in my drink. I hope you didn't take advantage of me."

"Ha, you wish. I thought you Geordies could drink. That was a poor performance."

"I'll make it up to you, I promise." I shout back.

I head to my room and spend the day chilling on my terrace. I keep out of the way of the girls, as I'm a tad embarrassed from last night.

On the second day of training, the gardens are delightful to see. The fresh air and summer breeze are perfect. I just smile and nod at the girls. I think they know I feel like a bit of an idiot getting carried away on day one.

The Architect appears from behind the trees, and he looks thrilled to see us.

"Welcome, students. I hope you are all adept at quieting the mind."

We all nod in sequence and listen in for day two. The Architect is holding court in the centre of the trees and spins to me.

"James, you're up first. The strength of all magical outcomes relates to four factors: belief, imagination, emotion, and clarity. You will enter gnosis, an altered state of consciousness where you will find the quiet to conquer the elements. This is one of your greatest tools for protection. Once mastered, you will be a force to be reckoned with. Please, James, take the centre of the grass and show us what you can do."

"Stand back, girls," I say eagerly, rubbing my hands and clearing my mind. I give them both a cheeky grin, as I'll do anything to impress them.

"OK, James, follow my lead." I stand quietly; I can feel a strange energy beginning to well up within me.

"Feel the power of the sun charging your heart, feel the earth ground you to the floor, and feel the wind as you master its power through your fingertips. Move water with your mind, imagine the sun sinking into a small star as it enters your heart."

"Now, James!" the Architect screams.

Uncontrollable energy bursts through the soles of my feet, traveling up my legs and the thirty-three vertebrae of my spine into my mind. Spinning wind circles at my fingertips, and lightning dances across the sky directly above me. My eyes flash with blinding white light. I drag the lightning down with my clutching right hand and throw it like a Yankees baseball pitcher.

The Architect and the girls dive out of the way, it crashes through the gardens onto a heavy, enormous World War II memorial bronze bell, waking up half of the city.

The Architect glances down at me and raises his voice.

"My patience is running thin. James, your ego will kill you one day if you don't listen to me. Now, move back and let the girls begin their practice."

They stand side by side in their satin cloaks with hoods up. They begin to levitate, hand in hand, in perfect formation, three meters off the grass, crashing their arms down like eagle's wings, exactly like my Uncle Crow did at the market.

Blue lightning sonic booms through the gardens tearing a huge tree in half, and a small fire breaks out. They both lift their arms together once more, bringing them down with such force that a ball of water crashes onto the burning trees and bushes, extinguishing them immediately.

The Architect jumps for joy, "Bravo, bravo, bravo!"

The adulation coming from him towards the girls pisses me off. Layla looks at me smugly and winks. It's obvious to me they've had plenty of training and are well-adept at magic. The day drags on as I lose my confidence, I'm no match for the girls and their natural ability. The Architect seems to judge my every move with his fiery glance. I can feel his beady eyes peering from his stupid hood, and it's wearing thin with me.

"That will be enough for today's practice. Girls, very well done." Turning to me with a stern look on his face, he mutters, "Do not cast your pearls before swine."

"What was that?" I mutter under my breath.

"Show me you're not expendable tomorrow with this cavalier attitude."

"You're joking," I reply.

"I don't joke. It seems you're the one that's blessed with charisma. Return to me at dawn tomorrow." He spins and marches off between the trees. What did I do to deserve that onslaught? He's been pushing me all day.

"Well done, girls, you are flying now. I feel like I'm drowning out there."

Layla puts her arm around me. "Don't worry, it will come. The more you lust after magic, the harder it is to manifest."

"I didn't understand his pearls riddle either."

"He's basically saying he won't waste his time if you don't appreciate it."

Layla is beautiful, and her aura shines so brightly. I tread carefully though, as she is a prolific flirt and a tease. It's late evening when The Architect releases us. Sky looks excited when we get back to Coven House.

"We are hitting the town, James. No excuses, you've got forty minutes to get your glad rags on."

I down a couple of freezing beers in the shower to take the edge off. I turn the knob, and icy water surges from the faucet, sending shivers cascading down my spine. Gently setting the empty bottle aside, I find myself hunched down, holding the front of my legs. I hope the power shower washes away any negativity from today's practice.

I splash on a strong, woody aftershave. I'm thinking, do I put double the amount on for two girls? I look along the wardrobe rail and pick a fitted, lightweight black suit with a bit of a flare on the trousers. Cuban heels with a wine-red bottom, a fitted white grandad shirt, and a black polka dot silk scarf tied in one knot, pushed inside the jacket.

I look in the mirror and know I'm not the same person I was from when I started my magical training. I hope that's a good thing.

Abracadabra, I'm ready for the town.

I spin out the door and head up to The Wheelhouse. The beautiful bright blue sky stretches endlessly above me. As I gaze at the sun disappearing over the historical buildings, I crush ice into my glass and pull myself a heavy measure of Honey Jack Daniels from the well-stocked bar. Gulping it down, it sends shivers down my spine.

I just want to forget about today. I blow thick dust off the record sleeve, placing it carefully on the turntable. The crackle and pop of *Pain* by The War on Drugs blasts across the rooftop — this is a perfect start to the evening.

After an hour's makeover, the girls emerge and strut onto the terrace. Someone certainly dressed them for the ball. My jaw drops at the magnificent sight. Both are dressed in identical, perfectly fitted black mini dresses, six-inch-high heels with never-ending lean legs, and deep red lipstick. They are a vision.

"Wow, James, you look like a rock star."

"Ha, funny bugger. I thought I'd make an effort."

Layla's perfect lips crash across mine. "Drink up, handsome," she purrs. "We are hitting the town."

We arrive at the vibrant waterfront of St. Julian's, where countless fishing boats bob gracefully in the grand harbour. Although it's a small fishing village, the promenade is breathtaking. The front of the bay is home to a cool Irish bar. The Guinness glasses crash down with shots of tequila. Layla flicks her hair and stares deeply into my eyes.

"It's one of those nights, James, where anything can happen."

The freezing Guinness hits the back of my throat, the shots line up, and Jimi Hendrix's *All Along the Watchtower* blasts through the bar. This is mine and my dad's favourite song. What a coincidence, but it was no time to be feeling sentimental and missing home.

We plough through trays and trays of drinks and dance into the night.

Sky and Layla sway to eighties electronic music, gazing into each other's eyes for just that moment too long. They know what they're doing to me as their bodies snake into each other. My mind goes blank, I'm suddenly outside on the pavement beneath the moon's gaze.

I can feel it dragging me like a powerful magnet in the sky. I hear my name getting screamed. The girls pile into the back of a taxi. "Come on, hurry, James!"

I dive straight into the back, and we take off into the deserted streets of St. Julian's.

We arrive back at Coven House, and the lust the three of us have for each other is too much to handle. They both lead me by each hand into my bedroom. A cool breeze blows across the room with the terrace doors wide open. Sky swings the bedroom door shut, running her hands through my hair. She shoves me hard backwards and I bounce onto the four-poster bed.

They both approach the bed, left to right on either side. Their mini dresses fall to the floor and their naked bodies glisten in the moonlight. They both fling themselves at me like the brides of Dracula, tearing my clothes off, entwined with thoughts of lust and shuddering ecstasy.

❖

CHAPTER 11

THE room is engulfed in a golden glow as sunlight pours through the veranda doors. My left eye opens, then the right. I'm not dreaming. I'm sandwiched in the middle of two naked goddesses. I wriggle free, trying not to wake them, and walk out onto the veranda naked. The hangover fairy has been, and I feel brand new. I'm looking forward to today's practice.

I gently shake Layla.

"Are you coming to practice?" I whisper. "You only have half an hour."

She groans. "Not today, James." Sky isn't moving either.

I'd better get my skates on; nothing a freezing shower and three strong espressos won't fix. The morning is magnificent as I approach the gardens. The Architect is sitting cross-legged on the lush grass, deep in meditation, enjoying the fruits of the baking sun. I doubt he's even in this dimension.

"Morning Architect!" I shout, trying to startle him.

"Good morning, James. Where are your companions?"

"Unfortunately, we had takeout food last night and we think they have a touch of food poisoning."

I don't enjoy lying for them, but I won't drop them in

it. He flashes me a wide smile and a nod, but I presume he sees through it.

"It looks like it's just us. We'll be working on manifestation and telepathy."

"Sounds good to me."

"We can walk and talk. I'll give you the grand tour of Valletta, as all of today's practice is in your mind."

We scale the city steps, leading us into Republic Square in the heart of Valletta, passing through the vibrant square full of holidaymakers and locals sharing their stories over an early breakfast. Tilting my head up to the queen, there's no sign of life. The Architect floats along in his robe, weaving us through the crowds, heading toward the city gate and away from the ancient walls.

We take a seat at the magnificent Triton Fountain, which serves as a captivating centrepiece, welcoming hordes of tourists. Walking tours gather in small pockets around the fountain area. Countless taxi drivers line the streets. Children play, and infants escape their parents' clutches. The fountain's cascading waters create a soothing sound, and the atmosphere is perfect.

"OK James, the secret to all manifestation is letting go of your desire. Once you have cast your spell, leave it in the universe's hands. Never come from a place of desperation or need. If you obsess over your magic and let it wander in your conscious mind, you won't reach your potential. You have the ability from your first day's training to quiet your mind and slip into the abyss."

I hang on his every word. I prefer the one-to-one approach of his teaching. His knowledge sinks in a lot better without the distraction of the girls.

"Are you keeping up? James, let me know if I'm being too esoteric. Let us walk."

We walk through the picturesque grounds of Parliament Square; it has a real sense of grandeur and importance. The cobblestone paving stones lead us through the grand arches of the Upper Barrakka Gardens, away from the vibrant energy of the surrounding streets.

Wandering through the peaceful ambiance, we step out onto the huge terrace overlooking the harbour with its jaw-dropping views. It's midday now, and soldiers reenact the gun salute at the battery. We take a seat on a bench as tourists gather, ready to listen to the gunfire. Kids play with the old silver binoculars, revealing boats disappearing into the horizon and the delights of the harbour.

"OK, James, telepathy is used for contacting fellow magicians from The Coven. We forbid it to be used on civilians, as they could not deal with this magic. We use it when talking to spirits, divine objects which we can bring back to life, such as statues and all animals."

The cannon's blast is a deafening fire, and The Architect is in his element.

"The art of telepathy is to focus on your chakras spinning. Say the words, EH-HEH-YEH out loud. Feel the vibration coming from that sphere and listen."

I hear his voice echoing in my mind.

"Are you hungry, James?" I turn to The Architect with wide-eyed amazement.

I burst out laughing.

"Shall we get lunch?" I fire back to The Architect's mind.

"Lunch is on me," he replies.

We wander back through the gardens, passing a grand statue of Saint John Valletta, and take a seat on the narrow, cobbled street at a fine Italian restaurant. As we settle into our seats, the aromas wafting from the kitchen start my stomach rumbling with the promise of fine cuisine. The charming waiter takes the lead and plies us with carefully selected white wine and the best lobster ravioli I've ever tasted - a culinary masterpiece.

"It's a perfect day. James, the reason I push you is to bring out the best in you. Don't think I'm picking on you because you've had no training. You have a gift, and you're adept in the great work. Magic runs through your veins. You just need to channel it correctly and not get distracted by the girls."

"Your task for tonight is to imagine an orange ball manifesting onto your terrace. You need to whisper the words, 'It is my will for an orange ball to arrive on my terrace without causing harm.' Push this into your subconscious when you enter the abyss."

We say our goodbyes for the day, and he hugs me the way my dad used to when we were close. I arrive back at Coven House. Layla skids past me and drops onto the sofa.

"So, tell me, how was your day with The Architect? Was he pissed?"

"Don't worry, I covered for you. I told him you were both sick from takeout food."

Springing up and kissing me on the cheek, she says, "You're a goody, James."

"Maybe you should swerve the drinks on a school night as you've missed the best day today?"

"OK, Dad," she hisses.

"If you miss a day, you could miss a piece of the puzzle." She doesn't reply. She just skips off to The Wheelhouse in her revealing red bikini.

I head to my terrace and follow The Architect's instructions to ask for an orange ball to arrive. Strange request, but he's the expert.

I take a cold shower and head to bed early.

I wake up with a jump. Layla has tiptoed into my room. I can see she's had the same nightmare on repeat. I rub my eyes.

"It's 3:30 a.m., you're keen."

"I just want a hug. I had a bad dream."

"It's the witching hour. If you're going to get pestered, this is the time the world opens up to entities on the astral, I heard The Architect mention it the other day."

The moon catches my eye; it looks strange in the night sky as it peers into my balcony.

"Just go to sleep. You'll need your rest for tomorrow." I pull my covers over my head. She must have something on her mind, as she snuggles into my back tightly.

The sun charges my body through the open terrace doors. I'm wide awake and ready to conquer the day. Layla has snuck off early, probably not to make Sky jealous.

I wander out onto my balcony, and looking down, I see a large orange children's football with a face painted on it, with a wide smile. I jump for joy. All I needed to do was let go, and it manifested.

❖

CHAPTER 12

I run into the warm wind, gliding through the open air in total harmony with nature, although sweat pours down my back and my forehead stinging my eyes. The warmth of the sun charges my body with every footstep. The gardens are another five hundred metres away, and the girls have left early, probably to suck up to The Architect for missing a day's training. I'm excited for today, and The Architect is full of beans.

"Welcome, students. I hope you are all prepared for today and have recovered." The girls answer with a patronising nod.

"OK, we are covering an advanced level of the lesser banishing ritual of the pentagram."

The three of us face east, overlooking the gardens. My mind is quiet. I don't have to draw the pentagrams with my hand. Bright blue pentagrams blaze around me in a complete magical circle. I look over to both girls, and they have a weak white rope circling them. The Architect claps excitedly.

"Bravo, bravo, bravo, James! Look at your pentagrams. This shows you have monstrous power."

Idle claps come from the girls. The Architect shares another pearl of wisdom.

"Your family, your friends, and society have always been telling you who you are. They've been telling you to fit in and to know your place. You are not here to fit in, you are here to stand out. Do you now see that all your decisions should always be your own?"

Today flies by, and we head back to the house. I can tell the girls' hearts aren't in it. As the sun shines in the sky, I dive into the shower. I pull on some black Versace gold iconic swim shorts that complement my tanned physique and head to The Wheelhouse to chill out for the rest of the afternoon.

The girls appear in matching black bondage style bikinis that leave nothing to the imagination, with the limited straps of material entwined around each of them. Layla shoots me a sharp glance and sinks into one of the sun loungers, hiding behind her Jackie Kennedy shades and white, oversized floppy hat. Sky runs at me like an Olympic gymnast, springing into the air and landing on me, binding her legs around my waist with a boa constrictor grip. My hands glide down, pulling her in closer.

"Well done, Mr. Merlin. You were amazing out there today. I'm so proud of you."

"Thank you, darling."

I gaze into her deep eyes and run my hand though her silky hair. She arches her back, leaning into me. She smells divine, like eucalyptus and sea salt. Our lips clash intensely, and she groans with pleasure, releases her grip, and jumps down.

"Enough of that for now, naughty. Fix us some drinks," she flashes me a cheeky smile. I follow her every footstep as she skips away, her perfect body in all its glory.

It's scorching on the terrace this afternoon. I rub some factor fifty sunscreen onto my head, as I am starting to look a tad red. Like a Geordie crabstick. I approach the girls with drinks tray high on my shoulder and a towel resting on my forearm.

As I approach Layla, I feel her body language is negative. I can see the irritation across her face. It's clear that something has gotten under her skin, and it looks like I'm in the firing line. I place her drink down next to her. She dips her sunglasses, and I know it's not going to be a thank you.

"You're becoming a proper teacher's pet, aren't you?"

I'm on my back foot now. "How do you mean?"

"Well, today's performance was the James show." She cocks her head and crosses her arms tightly. "You may have The Architect fooled, but I see straight through you."

I shake my head and just let her get things off her chest. She shifts her eyes towards me and begins her rant.

Sky looks on, gobsmacked.

"You're a sycophant who knows how to get his own way and perhaps you're afraid you're going to get beaten by a girl tomorrow. Imagine what that would do to your ego, James?"

"Don't flatter yourself, pet. You're good with your head start in magic and your constant practice, but the universe doesn't work hard, it just flows and that's what I'll do tomorrow to conquer battle magic."

She leaps up from her sun lounger, overcome with anger, and gets right into my face.

"Me and Sky will leave in a couple of days. I've seen this as a total waste of my time. I have a life in London to get on with."

"You know how to ruin a perfect afternoon, don't you? I suppose me and Sky will tread on eggshells the rest of this trip. Why don't you eat a bag of dicks and get out of my face?" I hiss.

"How dare you speak to me in that manner, you

northern monkey? I'm from a bloodline of kings and queens."

She storms off shouting at Sky, "Come on, you're too good for him."

Sky flashes me a concerned look and whispers, "Sorry," following the stupid cow.

Her words echo in my mind. What did she mean by my ego? I might be cocky, but I'm far from a narcissist.

I carry on serving gins to myself all day and playing a long list of classic Richard Ashcroft records. The day darkens, and the sun begins its slow descent behind the towering castle walls, casting a warm glow over the marina. I wrap up in a luxurious fur blanket, and a sense of comfort and security washes over me as I gaze at the superyachts, their lights flickering on all along the pier.

I daydream about Sky. Is this love that I'm feeling? I'm sure that's a Whitesnake lyric and a holiday romance spiralling out of control.

I wake up to an empty bed. It's been a while since I've had any visitors through the night. It's a glorious morning. I head down for breakfast, hoping to patch things up. I don't want to live like this. A wall of negative energy hits me once again as I approach the last few steps. I enter the lounge.

"What's with the gloomy faces?"

Layla doesn't look at me but mutters,

"You have a letter from The Coven."

The letter lies there, and you can feel the tension. She tosses it across the table. The red wax seal seems familiar. I open the elegant letter, ripping the wax seal to shreds. I try to hide my smile.

Reading aloud, "James, please attend day five alone and all three are to attend on the following Monday."

Layla jumps up and runs to her room. She swings her

door shut, and I jam my foot in the doorway to keep it from closing.

"Don't take this personally, it could mean anything."

"Out!" she screams like a banshee.

I head back into the lounge area; I know something is up. Sky doesn't even look up, sitting with her legs pulled against her chest.

"What the hell has gotten into her?" I ask.

She just shrugs her shoulders in bewilderment and blanks me. I feel sorry for Sky, as she's caught in the middle of this. I take off down the spiral stairs and run like the wind, leaving that shit behind me.

❖

CHAPTER 13

THE gardens are deadly quiet, as The Architect stares off into the harbour. I wonder what's going through his mind. His face lights up when he sees me.

"Welcome, James."

"Why am I here alone?" I ask.

"I feel the girls are insidious."

"How do you mean?" I'm shocked at what I'm hearing.

The Architect clicks his fingers and draws a circle of white light, cutting through the very fabric of the air, pointing at the centre with his index finger.

"Look, last night The SAF's elite inquisition spies arrived at the harbour."

The sleek elegance of a grey graphite gunboat cruises through the open waters, docking at Valletta harbour. Seven men step off the boat in matching suits and long grey macs. They march down the pier with military demure.

"How could Layla give up our location out of pure spite just because she isn't the centre of attention anymore?"

The Architect clicks his right fingers loudly and the edges of the circle start to blur and crackle. Energy spirals inward and the circle vanishes into thin air. He looks extremely disappointed, pulling down his hood.

"I chose Valletta because I knew it was a safe haven, and you could conquer the great work within these castle walls. They've put a hex on this whole expedition."

"All I can add is that Layla's eyes have changed over the last week back at the house, and she's heading down the left-hand path to black magic. It had to be her."

The Architect hands me a large brown leather-bound book with a pentagram engraved in the leather. It weighs a tonne and smells of distinct vanilla. Its cover is worn and weathered, as though it has been passed down through centuries, no doubt filled with magical treasures and esoteric knowledge.

"It's too dangerous to go back to Coven House for the next four weeks. I want you to go underground and study this book," he steps in closer, handing me a set of rusty old-fashioned keys, his voice taking on an assertive tone.

"Head to Birgu, it's a small fishing village over the water. There's a safe house just off the square. I want you to lie low there. I'll send for you once it's safe to return to Valletta and I've gotten to the bottom of this. Make sure you take a small fishing boat to Birgu so you're not picked up on any street cameras."

He hands me an identical robe to his.

"Wear this with your hood up and don't stop for anyone."

I quickly wrap the surrounding robe tightly and pull the hood up. I feel like a disciple of The Architect.

"Bravo, James, it looks good on you."

"Everything looks good on me," I say sarcastically.

"Be careful and Godspeed," he whispers.

We part ways, and once again, he vanishes through the trees.

Layla's treachery and betrayal knock me sick. I feel

gutted. I keep my head down and hood up, clutching the book tightly. I probably look like I'm on a pilgrimage to Rome in this outfit.

I approach the water's edge, looking over my shoulder every twenty meters to make sure I'm not being followed. A short, stocky, friendly fisherman with a bristly moustache and kind eyes invites me into his fishing boat.

"Birgu, please," I ask, crossing his hand with five euros in loose change.

I take a seat at the front of the boat; he bobs up and down, manning the oar as we chug along with his noisy little engine. We move swiftly across the water as it sprays my face gently, and the wind blows my hood down. I tightly clutch the book and think to myself that I'm fleeing on the water from The SAF once again.

Ten minutes later, the fisherman pulls up along the pier. I jump onto some stone steps and head up a steep bank, past a magnificent church that opens on to a small square.

The sunlight bathes the square in a peaceful glow, whilst weathered cobblestones guide me down a winding street into a quiet lane. Ahead, my eyes fall on an old-fashioned brown wooden door, its solid oak bearing the marks of time. To the right, a plaque reads 'Coven Heights,' and I know I've reached the safe house.

I reach into my robe for the old keys. Open sesame -turning the keys and releasing the solid bolts, top to bottom and at the centre of the door.

I let myself in and then turn to lock myself in my safe house.

It has a strange feel to it; there's nothing electrical, just an old library with dusty, ancient books under the stairs. It's dark and dated. You could call it traditional. I would call it bloody depressing.

A marble spiral staircase swallows the centre of the entire house. Looking up at the spiral centre, it's huge with five floors.

I scale the stairs to the first floor so I can escape easily through the roof window. I crash back onto the bed and rest my eyes for an hour or two.

The grandfather clock chimes 6 a.m. in the room's corner. I rub my eyes and double-take at the time — I've done it again; I've slept all the way through.

Church bells begin wailing from the main square, echoing through my narrow, winding street. I look down at the bed, and my legs are hanging off the bottom. I think they built it for a five-foot Maltese grandmother.

I spin the vintage wooden blinds to face the street. It's full of life. Locals shout, and scooters whizz past, beeping their horns. I take a quick shower and slip into a burgundy sports tracksuit. I'm comfortable and dressed to keep a low profile. I check the winding street and pull on a baseball cap and sunglasses.

It's safe to leave.

I take a seat at a nice little café on the corner of the square. The old waitress snakes through the tables, balancing far too many plates for my liking on her left arm. Her eyes light up when she takes my order, as she can't miss my northern twang.

"You're a long way from home, young man. What brings you to Birgu?"

"I'm just here with work."

"You staying long?"

"I'll see, maybe a few weeks." She quickly scribbles my order down and complains about the weather back home and how she would never return to Yorkshire.

The square buzzes with a friendly atmosphere. Old

people shuffle along and sit on park benches, exchanging stories of the day. I feel like I've stepped into an old black-and-white movie. Hours pass as I sit, sipping coffee and people-watching. Back in Newcastle, I was the one with all the answers. Here, I have none. I stare into space, fantasizing about being back on the doors, running my dad's empire, playing my records at home, and chilling with Nipper.

Simpler times. I'd give my right arm for them.

Like a modern-day Spartan, I keep a routine and control my life. I'm up before the church bells every day, meditating on the rooftop with the "together breath," losing myself in a trance. I keep myself fit and battle-ready, scaling up and down the spiral stairs of the five floors.

An old, taped-up leather punching bag that's seen more rounds than Rocky Marciano hangs on the rooftop. I grunt with every shot, peppering the bag, moving through every combination, then wail down thunderous Thai kicks, nearly chopping the bag in two. I lose count of the hours and the rounds I spend destroying the bag, ending up in a heap every day, drenched in sweat on the cold marble floor.

My muscles ache all over in this burning heat. I'm probably overtraining. Every day feels like a lesson, and with each one, I'm getting better and better. But I'm not sure how much longer I can keep up this routine.

Beneath the stairs, there is a small library, and I devour every single book. I find myself drawn to elemental magic, and before long, I've mastered the great work. In no time, I study Thelema, Crowley's teachings, the Kabbalah, and mysticism from cultures around the world.

I eat at the same corner cafe every day, so I'm familiar with my surroundings. It's nice to chat with the owner and the staff to keep me sane. I take a seat on the corner, nestled away within the charming square. Parasols flutter in the wind, providing sanctuary from the baking sun. The comforting smell of rich coffee fills my nostrils as I soak up the ambiance.

Old-looking mafiosos sit by themselves, wearing two-inch-thick Roy Orbison shades and itchy-looking lamb's wool cardigans in the baking heat. They follow the same routine, drinking espresso and strong liquor all day long, occasionally tipping their flat caps to acquaintances but never budging for anyone.

I sit on the roof in the evenings, a far cry from the luxury of The Wheelhouse at Coven House. The skies are filled with endless washing lines of crumpled hanging clothes.

I miss the girls and their contagious laughter, their continuous flirting.

A few weeks have passed. I have food and shelter, the sun shines from dawn to dusk. But without anyone to share it with, I am incredibly lonely. I'm a social butterfly and I'm not used to being on my own this long. I stare into the gaping void, and there's still no sign of The Architect.

❖

CHAPTER 14

TODAY I stand alone by my bedroom window, overlooking the square, with only the church bells to keep me company. The days crawl by as I wait for The Architect to reach out and rescue me. I'm going out of my mind.

I peer through the blinds, watching the tourists and locals with envious eyes, longing for some company.

My Spartan routine has slowly gone out the window, and I've become something else – a vampire, sleeping all day, downing bottles of rum through the night in a voodoo mist, practicing magic.

I head through the cobbled, windy streets toward the square. The sun is high in the sky, and there's not a cloud in sight. I'm running out of provisions, and the shops close at midday.

I approach a small shop that looks like an Aladdin's cave stocked with everything, from cleaning products to electric toys, floor to ceiling. Everything is written in Italian. I can't work out what I'm buying.

The shop owner looks about two hundred years old, her mahogany skin glowing under the dim lights.

"Is this washing up liquid?" I ask.

She just nods and smiles. In the end, I make out that it's floor cleaner.

I'm running low on money, so I stick to a tight budget—booze, fresh crusty bread rolls, and cheese spread. I'm pretty sure that counts as part of your five-a-day.

I keep my head down as I pass the coffee shop on the corner, just shuffling past without making eye contact.

I drink myself into oblivion every day. I think about my family and hope they're safe.

A full moon looms over Birgu on this eerie night. My candles flicker in the dark corners of the front room. I know I have real magic ability. I'm an innovator, fearless.

Sky told me she'd always loved the Roald Dahl quote: "Those who don't believe in magic will never find it."

I begin, casting a makeshift circle with some cooking salt to keep me safe. I've read horror stories about stepping outside your protective circle. The Architect's grimoire warns in bold writing: "Never trust a spirit or entity fully, for they are always jealous of your divine spark."

I draw blue flaming pentagrams with my index finger North, East, South, and West—surrounding me, and vibrate the words, "AH-TAR! Show me thy spirit for whom I have cast."

The rhythmic chanting of my voice echoes off the damp walls. The room grows freezing and still. The cold stone floor is harsh against my bare feet, sending a chill through my body and making the hairs on the back of my neck stand on end.

My black-and-white twin altar candles flicker, faintly casting a dim glow over the sacred circle. The light barely touches the area.

Then, a voice whispers my name - "James" - in my right ear. The sound sends a shiver straight up my spine.

Suddenly, my altar candles explode over a metre high,

knocking me back in fright. The room grows icy cold, now filled with a sinister energy.

A spirit appears outside my blue flaming circle.

"Hello, James, my name is Astrid. I've been watching you for a long time. It's nice to finally meet you."

She could be an Indian princess, with long, shiny hair, olive skin, and sparkling blue eyes. Her voice is soft, almost hypnotic.

"Why do you wallow in desperation? What is it that you desire so deeply?"

"I just want to go home," I reply, my voice thick with frustration. "I'm sick of this life, locked up in here."

"Do not fret. I am here for you now," she says soothingly. "Why do you stand in the centre of the circle? I won't bite you."

I feel her eyes heavily on mine as if she's reading my mind.

"Who told you to stand inside your circle?"

"The Architect is my mentor."

"Ah," she sighs. "It looks like The Architect has abandoned you," laughing creepily.

The sound sends a ripple of unease down my spine.

I instinctively take a step back, my discomfort rising.

"OK, James, when you're ready to join me, cross over to this side and I'll do your bidding. I can manifest any desire or riches for you. You just need to make a pact with me. How about I bring the contract next time you evoke me? Let's say, tomorrow evening at the same time?"

"I need to think about this." I reply nervously.

Her voice raises angrily. The flames on the candles burst uncontrollably. Her voice raises angrily. "Act fast," she snaps, lunging forward but unable to enter the now sacred circle. Thank God.

"Do you know how many mortals would love to be in your shoes? Even speaking to me is a great honour," she hisses.

Locking her eyes on me like prey, she adds, "You have twenty-four hours. You don't need to live in squalor. Put yourself first and live gloriously."

She flickers and flickers, then disappears back into the veil. The candles shrink instantly, and the room brightens up.

I fall in a heap, although the room is freezing, I am drenched in sweat.

It's safe to leave the circle now, so I head out for a walk down to the harbour. I zip up my tracksuit and pull my cap low, covering my eyes. The marina has a peaceful stillness on the water's edge. I wander with my hands in my pockets like a lost soul for about half a mile.

Birgu harbour is full of beautiful boats rocking back and forth. I stop at a busy open-air bar called The Harbour Inn and order a Bloody Mary from a pretty Eastern European waitress. The bar is bustling with crew from the boats and groups of happy-go-lucky girls dolled up for the night.

I used to be the centre of attention everywhere I went. Now, I sit in the corner with a huge beard and sunken eyes, wearing a sports tracksuit that I wouldn't even walk the dog in back home. I sit sipping a Bloody Mary, listening to people's conversations from neighbouring tables. The more I drink, the more I think about joining Astrid and living gloriously as I stumble along the pier, just making it up the bank square.

An ancient church's light shines down, illuminating my path and making my journey back home a bit easier. I'm not sure what to think about Astrid's offer, it seems the only thing I have going for me in these dark times.

I awake feeling like I've turned a corner, and it's time to

clean up my act. Looking into the mirror, my reflection tells a story of months of stress and hard living. Life is essentially about how I react to situations and how I deal with them.

I scrub the house from top to bottom. Hours pass as I fall into a cleaning trance, burning white candles throughout the home to clear any negative energy. I finish with ten rounds on the bag, smashing it to bits before moving on to an intense grooming mission.

The beard is gone, revealing a clear, tanned, youthful face. Light shines again in my eyes. The expensive navy-blue suit hanging up fits me like a glove as I glide into the jacket. I tie a Windsor knot with the expensive-looking tie, and instantly, I feel a sense of purpose.

The whole day flies by in a heartbeat. It's approaching 7 p.m. I run my right hand through my long, blonde, sun-bleached hair and step into my protective circle.

I stand in the centre, and a ray of flaming blue pentagrams engulfs me. I vibrate the words again: "AH-TAR! Show me thy spirit for whom I have cast."

Astrid appears instantly, with a charming, wide smile and beautiful, sparkling eyes. A long silk dress flows perfectly showing off her ravishing figure.

"Hello James, it's nice to see you again."

A contract floats outside the circle looking like an old sea scroll unravelling down in deep red ink, hovering before my eyes.

I scan the contract from left to right. It reads:

'Mr. James Gunner, to fulfil his contract to have any wishes granted in exchange for thy soul.'

I give it a once-over, shaking my head firmly; I know this would be a grave mistake. She stares at me intensely, her voice rising.

"Well then, James, are you excited to join me?" The

grim tale behind her eyes makes me shiver. I see through her contract—she's creepy, twisted, and perverted.

"I'm sorry, but this does not interest me."

Her eyes hypnotize me, and my feet begin to edge toward the outer circle. I shake myself awake quickly. Her face flickers, and her eyes turn deathly red, an inhuman look crossing her features.

"Not interested!" she screams.

A crackle of energy breaks the following silence, and a tremendous flash of thunderous light bursts through the room filling every nook and cranny, knocking me off my feet.

Candle flames explode over two meters high all around me. The tone of her voice deepens and vibrates. "I'll be watching you, and when you fall into this pit again your signature and soul will be mine."

Vanishing in an instant, I'm left in a heap on the cold floor, drenched in sweat. I loosen my tie and slip it off my neck. A sense of achievement washes over me as I have turned her down. I'm not some weak, pathetic man to be manipulated. I am a sorcerer of great power.

❖

CHAPTER 15

A few days have passed since my bizarre encounter with the spirit, Astrid. I've been here for months now, cut off from my friends and family. I've considered my alternatives carefully, but I've been in this house too long. It's time to return to Valletta. If I can't find anyone from The Coven, I'll stow away on a boat to mainland Europe.

I make my way to the local coffee shop for breakfast. I sit facing the square and order an espresso with fresh salmon and scrambled eggs. A toddler, no older than three, bounces over to my table. His chubby little face cheers me up. He looks directly at me, and his vibrant, playful eyes suddenly transform into something terrifying - glazed fully black. The blackness pulls me into a trance.

The sinister melody of his deep unearthly voice sends shivers down my spine. He growls,

"I have a message for you James, he's watching and waiting!"

I jump back in my seat in fright and spill my espresso on my lap. The toddler's mother gives me a dirty look and snatches her child away, muttering something in Maltese under her breath. I probably look like a total freak.

I leave a twenty euro note in a hurry, this haunting encounter seems to linger in the air as I race back to the safe house.

Later that day, I make my escape. I flag a cab on the square and travel through the winding streets, passing the monstrous castle walls, before arriving at Theatre Street.

I jump out of the taxi, met by the buzzing energy of the long, cobbled streets, filled with endless bars, charming cafés, chic little restaurants, and cool little hippy shops.

I start the night at a proper old-style, London-style bar, The Queen's Head. It's four deep at the bar, but I manage to get a table in the corner, not wanting to draw attention to myself.

I have a perfect view of the large, tiled entrance. A waitress in a gothic black leather jumpsuit, platforms, and peculiar makeup takes my order of Guinness and nachos. The place has a friendly atmosphere, with holidaymakers, stag and hen parties, and locals partying the night away.

I head outside for some fresh air. The air is still warm and soft, though the moonlight spills onto the cobbled street. Something keeps me grounded on the cobblestones.

I hear a posh English accent behind me.

I should have kept moving. A man in a long grey mac was staring at me. I could sense something sinister in the air. The warm wind caught his long grey Burberry mac, making it flutter slightly.

I fixate on the small Japanese Katana sword tucked away inside his belt. I quickly look away but keep my cool.

There's no way I can run. A shudder runs through me as he opens his mouth.

"Excuse me, sir, have you seen this man?"

To my dismay, it's an A4 mugshot of me. I don't even make eye contact. I just bolt down the back lane.

Footsteps pound behind me.

"Stop!" They scream, "I command you to stop!"

I glance over my right shoulder. Six men in long, grey macs are on me like a cheap suit. We spill into St. George's Square. It's completely dark.

I navigate by the cloud-covered moon, using it as my compass, but the footsteps are getting louder. I thought I was fast, but these men have been highly trained; they're in peak condition. I glance back, and the leader's blade shines in the moonlight as he draws it from its sheath. My body is a vessel of insane powerful energy.

Each chakra is spinning at full speed, like pulsating wheels, my heart leaping out of my chest.

They're closing in, covering too much ground, hot on my heels. The leader is only six feet away, raising his sword high in the sky, ready to strike.

I recognize the street where I had lunch with The Architect. I know I can escape into the gardens ahead.

The only thing I can see as I sprint down the back lane is a colossal statue of Jean de la Valette, the Grand Master of the Knights of Saint John. I clear my mind and ask for help. If they catch me, I'm dead.

"Please help me, someone come to my aid."

A stern voice echoes in my mind, "Draw them in closer to me, my boy."

We approach a tight corner and the statue of Jean de la Valette bursts from his pedestal with all his might. He headbutts the first and runs his long sword straight through him. The SAF spy buckles, coughing up blood and crashes to the floor.

The spies look horrified as he calmly wipes the blood from his sword onto his puffy sleeve. He looks directly at me and smiles,

"Run, James. I'll hold them off."

Four men unleash their Katana swords and charge at him. He ploughs through them like a force of nature. I've never witnessed such brutality. Crude headbutts smashing and blood-curdling sword strikes, tearing through the air. I'm frozen, standing in a trance.

"Run," he commands. I'm on my toes now.

The city gate is a sharp right. I can make it to the taxis lined up ahead at the fountains.

I come to a breathless halt at the gate. A spy skids to a stop at the far end of the bridge, blocking my path.

He slowly undoes his grey mac and shows his sword.

"You have two options," he barks. "You can have this sword deep in your gut or you're coming back to England with me."

He looks like a ruthless, evil bastard. His eyes are void of empathy, and I know I can't trust him. All that these robots do, is follow orders.

"I'll take the sword please," I reply firmly.

A great surge of power erupts within me, lifting my chest as adrenaline floods my veins. I'm in fight-or-flight mode now. He draws his sword violently and sprints towards me with a battle cry.

A flash of sparkling steel slices through the air toward my crown. I jump to the left with perfect timing and stamp my right foot into his chest plate, kicking him over the gate.

His screams echo hauntingly as he plummets a hundred feet to his death. I can't bring myself to look. I know there's no way he could have survived the fall, crashing onto the jagged rocks below.

I feel a tight curdling in my stomach and fall to my knees, violently expelling the Guinness I'd just downed.

My eyes are streaming, and I'm hunched over in a pool of luminous sick and blood. The cut on my wrist is pouring of blood. The spy's sword must have just caught it, it's left behind a four-inch gaping wound.

A large, imposing figure stands over me.

"Rise, you fool, celebrate his death. They sent him here to slaughter you."

I wipe the bitter sickness from my lips and drive myself to my feet.

"Thank you for helping me."

I pick out my handkerchief from my upper pocket and press hard on the wound. It wouldn't hold for long. I needed medical attention, but I couldn't go to the hospital.

"Thank you again."

He flashes me the widest, friendliest smile.

"You're welcome! I've stood in the same spot for a hundred years. It can get boring, just getting your photo taken every day by swarms of tourists."

I half-laugh as he spins off, shouting over his shoulder.

"You can call on me anytime you run into trouble in these city walls. You have the divine spark to bring me back, so I am always in your debt."

I take off at high speed down the back streets, sweat pouring down my back as I pass enormous sandstone political buildings with grand, solid double doors. I fly down hundreds of stairs, retracing the path where my journey began. I approach the entrance to the gardens, a pang of sadness hitting me as I think about the fun I had at Coven House with the girls. It's getting late, and I'm growing more concerned about my wound.

There's a shadow behind an old tree. I'd recognise that heavy cotton robe anywhere. The sight nearly makes me burst into tears.

The relief is overwhelming, and I just collapse into him.

"Where have you been?" I screech.

"You probably think it was all a test, but you've excelled beyond words."

I hold on to him tightly, fighting back the tears. The metallic smell of blood fills the air as my handkerchief falls to the floor. The Architect clicks his right fingers, and white light bursts from his fingertips.

He zips his fingers along my wound, stitching the fibres together as if I'd never been hurt. The pain vanishes instantly.

"Unfortunately, James, I must leave you."

"How do you mean? We've just been reunited."

I release my grip and push him back, lost for words. He smiles at me, pulling down his hood.

"You turned down the contract to wicked evil sorcery. Few would have been able to resist signing under the pressure you faced. But I cannot protect you on this plane. Mortals must find their own way. These are the divine rules, above and below. The angels can guide you, but my time is up here."

It batters my head. We're back in the beautiful gardens, and it feels like day one all over again.

He clicks his fingers, and a six-foot circular portal bursts into existence, rippling with insane energy. His last words give me the answers I've been seeking.

"Everyone must follow their own journey. Life is but a series of tests toward enlightenment until you return to the sky." He steps into the portal, and blinding white light engulfs him.

"I can always find you, James. You shine like a diamond in the darkness of the sky."

The portal swallows him up, pulling him into the unknown. A cold tear trickles down my face.

Standing between the mighty trees, I feel a sense of pride and connection with nature. But doubts linger. Will my magic still hold its power without The Architect's presence?

❖

CHAPTER 16

I need to drum up support from the spirit world and get the angels on my side. I had heard about a psychonaut named Cosmic Frank. He lives on the other side of the island in a trendy part called Sliema and he's known as the Malta Mystic.

Every morning, he practices yoga at dawn and swims in the old Victorian rock pools in the sea. It's scorching today, and the sun cracks the pavement. I take a small fishing boat from Birgu to the lower ferry port of Valletta.

I keep my baseball cap low, hiding my face, sweat trickles down my back, it's that hot. The ferry is deadly quiet with it being before 7 a.m. We sail along on its first journey of the day.

I have amazing views from the roof and the waterway is packed with boats that look like old ghost ships docked and left behind. The warm wind is relaxing as we approach the pier of Sliema. A friendly ticket inspector points along the rocks, giving me directions to the Victorian pools.

I take a light jog along to wake my body up for around a mile. I can see Cosmic Frank up ahead. It must be him. He's the only person on the front. Twisting and bending into peculiar yoga moves. He was of medium height, average build, with a foot long, black, tight, curly Afro that looked like a sundial.

He greets me with a friendly face.

"Excuse me, are you Cosmic Frank by any chance?"

"Yes, that's me," he replies in a strong Geordie accent. "I see you're from Newcastle as well."

"Ha, I thought you were a local?"

"I was born and bred on Walker Road, bonny lad or when I'm trying to impress anyone it's upper Quayside. I landed in the eighties but kept missing my plane home, so I just stayed."

He rips his psychedelic shirt off over his head and, with a crooked, crazy smile, sprints and dives off the rocks, plunging into the rough sea. I quickly strip down to my boxer shorts and follow him in at speed, bombing into the freezing, refreshing water.

The waves are enormous as they pound onto the rocks. We bob up and down a few meters from each other.

"What can I do for you, young man?"

"The SAF chased me from Newcastle all the way here; I escaped capture last night."

His Afro has collapsed by now, which looks comical.

"It's nice to speak to someone from back home. I've missed the people and the banter."

Cosmic Frank tips his head under the water and explodes back up over a huge crashing wave.

"They will return with reinforcements," he shouts over the waves.

"Without a doubt. I have little time on my hands. I thought I could drum up support from the spirit world?"

He front crawls away a few metres and, using the metal ladder steps attached to the Victorian rock pools, pulls himself up back onto the promenade, jumping up and down to dry himself off. "Of course, I'll help a fellow Geordie," he shouts.

That was music to my ears. My arms glide through the water with a powerful front crawl. I launch myself out of the water and blast up the ladders onto the promenade to hear his proposal.

"The only way you're going to get to that place is by the vine of the dead, Ayahuasca. The only people who have access to it on this island are Sonny and Cher."

I think he's joking about the name. He hands me a black and white business card with bold white writing and a number consisting of seven threes on it.

"Call this number today and you'll be on the other side within twenty-four hours." He reaches out his hand and strangely has an iron grip for a man with his build.

"Thank you, it's been nice to see a friendly face. Look me up if you ever return to Newcastle. I run The North Star for my dad."

His extreme laughter breaks free and fills the air with joy around us.

"You're not Raymond Gunner's son, are you?"

"I am."

"Well, I'm here to support you. I remember mad Ray from back in the day. They don't make men like him anymore."

Once again, strangers know more about my father's past than I do. I bid Cosmic Frank farewell and take off along the Sliema promenade. A black tarmac cycle path winds all the way along the front, past many cool cafes and tourists. I finally find an old, battered phone box, I'm surprised it's still working. I call the number on the card, quickly punching in the digits. I listen to the ringtone nervously.

A deep and melodic voice answers. "Sonny here, speak!"

"Hi, I've been given your number by Cosmic Frank."

"Ah, Frankie boy," he replies.

"I need to book in for Ayahuasca as soon as possible."

"How soon?"

"I mean tonight?"

"Well, you're in luck. We've had a cancellation. You follow a strict diet for seven days to get the best possible results, so that's on your toes. I'm at the Sliema Mall apartment complex on the front, above the main gym. We're in the penthouse. I'll see you at 5 p.m. and bring four hundred euros." The line goes dead.

That's practically going to clean me out, but I must take the chance. I have a few hours to kill. At the front of the restaurant is a sign that says, "Open air fish restaurant with superb views of the sea."

I spend the whole day in peace, in a trance, simply watching the many boats sail in the wind. I sip sparkling water, observing the prestigious yacht race. Each sail flashes a different bright tropical colour in a fierce battle for the winning position. It's incredibly entertaining to watch.

I ask a busy waiter for directions, and to my surprise, I'm directly in front of Sonny's building. I head off, and it's only a five-minute walk through a narrow, cobbled street.

I press the intercom of a flashy, enormous glass door, and a friendly voice answers.

"Hi, it's James. I spoke to you this morning."

"Of course, you're right on time. I'll buzz you in."

I enter an elegant gold-panelled mirrored lift that takes me directly to their private floor. After exiting the lift, I ring the doorbell of the solid orange oak front door. Sonny greets me with a magic smile and a loving hug and whispers,

"Welcome, brother."

Sonny is of medium height and build, with bright

brown eyes. The apartment is open plan with multiple carpets on the wooden floors, makeshift beds out of many blankets, a bucket to purge any negativity from your body, and bottles of water lined up. Blackout curtains cover the balcony doors, stopping any light from breaking through. The only light comes from the many flickering red candles burning throughout.

"Meet Cher, my beautiful wife."

I'm greeted with another warm, perfect hug. Cher has beautiful, dark, naturally curly hair, perfect olive skin, and sparkling jade eyes. It's hard to guess how old they are with such fun, vibrant energy blasting from the pair of them. She's wearing a long witchy dress that flows elegantly to the floor, it trails behind leaving an aura of mystique and refinement.

"Welcome to our home, James. We will both be your guides today. You have nothing to worry about. This is a perfectly natural experience. Do you have any questions?"

A nervous tension suddenly begins to echo in my stomach, though to me it sounds like a foghorn, I doubt they can hear it, but I don't want to give anything away.

We enter the ritual floor space in the centre and take a seat on the pink Indian chequered blanket to begin our journey. A cauldron has been bubbling away the whole day with the vines of Ayahuasca. Sonny carefully drains the substance into a cup. He hands me the Holy Grail as I down the magic potion.

It shudders through my body, gagging at what tastes like swamp water, as it stings my eyes and almost pours from my nostrils. Sonny and Cher, both take theirs together in perfect timing and systematically blow candles out around us. It's pitch black now, and I can only make out the outlines of their faces through the dim candlelight.

Sonny blows smoke all around my body to free negative energy and to bring protection. We all sit with our hands in a prayer grasp, and Cher leads us in with her soothing voice that pours into my ears. Thanking God for all he has done for us in our lives, I feel grateful and happy. I nearly jump out of my skin as Cher whistles into a bottle, the sound echoing throughout the room.

"Is everybody in? Let the ceremony begin!"

Like a small child hiding from the monsters that lurk in the shadows, I wriggle in comfort under a blanket. There is a strange energy pulling me through the floor. I get frightened and sit up quickly.

I try to fight the plant as its vines entwine around me, creeping up my body slowly and around my neck into my mind. Sonny is rattling leaves like an Indian witch doctor.

The room drops into a distinct vibration and frequency.

Looking over at the sofa, I can sense its true composition. It's as though I'm witnessing the very fabric of the universe before me. Numbers and geometric shapes flicker and come together in intricate patterns. The way all the elements of the furniture align to form solid matter is truly spectacular. I rise, just as a vine is about to reach my mouth, pulling me toward the covers and drawing me into rest.

Sonny asks, "Are you OK?" in a reassuring voice.

"I'm not sure."

"Why are you whispering in the dark?"

"I'm scared. May I have some more protective smoke?" He jumps up as though he can see in the dark and blasts smoke down my back. Choo Choo Choo, it performs a mystical dance, wrapping itself around me in a soothing hug. I feel calmer as he takes his seat, and they sing a hymn to bring Ayahuasca into the room, banging loudly on the ancient drums.

What am I seeing? Their faces have changed. I'm no longer in the room with Sonny and Cher. It's something else, and I don't want to hang around to let my conscious mind decide for me. I surrender to Ayahuasca and whisper.

"Take me."

With my arms across my chest like an Egyptian mummy, I fall backwards into the floor. I fall and fall into the darkness. I'm gone. Will I ever return to Sonny and Cher's front room?

I am weightless, tumbling into the black space. Nothing but darkness lures me in, deeper and deeper now, spiralling into the darkest abyss. As I plummet into the darkness, it seems to devour everything in its path.

The black space fills my body with excruciating fear and anxiety. The fabric changes quickly from black smooth silk into alien crystal shards of glass. I land at a sudden halt. I'm now standing in an evil, crippling realm. I know this place isn't human. It's unnatural, a cursed place. Alien faces pull through the crystals with silent screams that haunt me. All I can do is close my eyes tightly.

My chakras don't work down here, and I've lost the magical power from my fingertips. The feeling of doubt and fear swallows me up. What have I done? I wouldn't wish this on my worst enemy. I always wondered what death would feel like if you hadn't reached your true potential, drifting through life would undoubtedly lead to this place of truly lost souls.

Ayahuasca teaches me a brutal lesson for what feels like hours, a crushing sensation. I hear a great rumble, and out of the crystals, a colossal figure is upon me. He commands my attention.

"Mr James Gunner, I am Osiris, the God of the underworld, welcome. You have courage coming to this realm of your own accord. I knew it wasn't your time to officially visit."

His evil ruby-red eyes peer from his great Egyptian gold helmet into my heart and mind, with timeless knowledge and wisdom that reach an existence from when the very first words were spoken into creation. His emerald and gold armour is so bright, it blinds me as he approaches. He thumps his enormous golden staff down, sending echoes through the crystal realm.

"How may I be of service to you?" he booms.

I hesitate to tell him about my reasons for traveling here. I need as much help as I can but working with good and evil at the same time doesn't sit right with me. I need to get out of here.

"Have you gone deaf, fool? Why do you travel to the underworld to be judged before your time?"

Closing my eyes tightly, I say the ritual in my head.

"Before me Rafael, behind me Gabriel, on my right-hand Michael, on my left-hand Uriel. I call on thee to protect me!"

Time seems to have evaporated and reveals itself as an illusion. The brightest angelic white light shines down on me. Osiris pulls his staff to protect him. The Archangels crash down, made from castle rock, circling me like a wishing well.

Raphael shouts.

"Look up James. We don't have the power to hold him off." A beautiful, soft voice appears in my mind telepathically.

I feel I can trust her voice.

"Reach up to me, James, quick - take my hand."

Osiris roars with anger, approaching the light, screaming, "You will belong to me one day, mark my words, so mote it be!"

The powerful white light swallows me up as I grip the

lady's hand with deep intensity. We blast off into a tunnel engulfed in peace and love.

Every particle in my body is at one with the white light. Spiralling through space and time, we head out into the universe. The wind flies through my hair as we blast off. A new planet, untouched by man, emerges—a perfect planet with clear blue skies, deep green forests, and magical lakes and seas.

The lady points down to a golden bright light. Her voice vibrates in my mind again.

"Look James, it's Galantion, the city of love and light." I've never seen such beauty. I am mesmerised.

"What is it?" I gasp.

"It's your birth home. Your soul will return there one day to your ancestors. Ask anything you desire."

"Am I on the right path? I need to know if I'm doing the right thing."

"Follow your heart, and it will lead you to your glory," she says peacefully. She lets go of my hand, and I drift through space, past so many unrecognisable planets full of dazzling colours.

I land in a great, powerful, warlord's body, standing on a mountaintop in fox furs. I look down on my tribe as they sit around the fire. The crackling flames jump and dance in the darkness, in tune with the beating drums. An Indian shaman moves to the beat, stamping sand, telling us a story in his sacred dance. Many beautiful Native American wives pull my furs off, revealing my naked body and I'm led into the master wigwam. The fruits of their desires are denied as I blast into the sky again.

I am now an eagle soaring through the clouds. Totally free, my wingspan is colossal. Ayahuasca has shown me both sides of the coin. From darkness to light, I soar and glide down. I land on a horse trotting along, dressed in a full black and red samurai battle outfit. I wonder if this is all my past lives. I gallop faster, bringing up thick dust. I'm traveling at such speed I can't see a thing, and bang—I crash forward onto Sonny and Cher's floor. I gasp as though I've taken my first breath, drowning in Ayahuasca.

"Welcome back, James."

"What the hell? How long have I been away?"

"You've been gone for five hours." A great rumble in my stomach curdles. "Don't worry, there was no old witchcraft, curses, or hexes in your body. I pulled nothing from your back," Sonny shouts.

I jump up and run to the toilet. The bucket is next to my bed. I'm not purging out of my mouth. I just make it to the toilet, crashing down onto the seat. The world falls out of my rear, letting out screams. Around eight litres of negative energy, as murky evil water, falls like the Hoover Dam walls have given in. I flush with my elbow, drenched in sweat, holding onto the seat for dear life. Another four litres surge out.

All my regrets from my past disappear down the toilet bowl. All my anxiety about the future vanishes; I laugh hysterically, wiping the sweat away from my forehead.

I've made it back in one piece. I am reborn.

❖

CHAPTER 17

I was on top form from my Ayahuasca experience, a perfect week had drifted by. I feel like I've found out the meaning of life but forgot to write it down. It doesn't matter, though. I'm a blank canvas, and I like what I see in the mirror.

I have forgiven myself and moved on; it's time to face the music as I travel to Valletta. News would have reached The SAF by now, as the spies haven't checked in, and I've evaded capture. All the pieces of the puzzle have come together, and it's become clear I must go on the journey alone.

Beneath the high sun, I arrive eagerly at the grand city gate. I quickly put on my sunglasses. There isn't a cloud in the bright, beautiful blue sky. I'm walking at a fast pace past a huge line of taxis at the fountain and enter the upper gardens. I smile, thinking about the day I shared with The Architect.

The fountain waters flow peacefully as I head through an enormous grand sandstone archway, with grassy greens on the left and right, and countless large, wise old trees. A tiled walking path leads me to the panoramic views of the grand harbour. It was nearly midday, and I looked down to the next level. Soldiers prepare to reenact the gun salute, which serves as a defensive and ceremonial platform. Gunfire will greet anyone of importance as they arrive at the harbour. They dress in bright red, immaculate uniforms with white custodian helmets. They look amazing as they stand to attention, proud of their history and their role.

I take a seat on a wooden bench overlooking the harbour. The sun's golden rays bounce off the bright blue waters, sparkling as they're covered in gigantic super yachts and tiny turquoise and canary yellow fishing boats. If I wait any longer, the boats will make me think of my escape, and I'll have to do it soon. The North Sea would be too unforgiving and treacherous to cross in the late autumn.

The only thing I have in my possession is the Talisman ring. I glance down at the red ruby sparkling from the sunlight on my little finger. It seems to come alive as my gaze lingers. There's no way I can sell it just for a ticket home. Who knows what would come from calling on its power?

I head over to the sandstone walls, looking out at the mesmerising sea. There's a long line of dots in the distance. I place a coin in the side of some old, battered, rusty silver binoculars and manoeuvre them with the handles on either side, focusing on the line of dots.

The lenses clear and I watch in wide-eyed terror as a vast fleet of SAF forces approaches at speed. I turned the handles towards me and zoomed in on the leading boat.

A grey graphite battleship charges toward the Valletta harbour, leaving wave after wave behind. To the left and right, small people carrier boats are jam-packed with SAF special forces and horses. The lead boat is a naval masterpiece, sleek with Gatling gun turrets on every corner that could cut through anything. The sound of the drums echoes through the air and across the water, flooding me with anxiety. As they prepare to impose their demonic force, the drums grow louder and louder. The binoculars reveal a systematic line of five naval boats on either side of the lead, and a fleet of seven backup gunships around twenty minutes behind, waiting for their chance to leap into action.

The drums beat in my chest, setting off the chakras in my body from the soles of my feet to my mind's eye.

I quickly levitate down twenty feet to the next level to get a closer look at what I'm about to deal with.

Landing gracefully in front of the two acting soldiers, they sprint off in horror, the sound of their military helmets bouncing to the floor. The group of tourists who witnessed my flying trick leave in a hurry.

I'm left by myself with the drums pounding in my ears as the battleship sails into the harbour, followed by a single file of people carrier boats packed with hundreds of troops.

I quickly look behind and, to my surprise, a line of eight cannons stands proudly, protecting the harbour against a naval assault. Twenty cannonballs are neatly stacked in perfect form next to each gun.

The gunboats sail into the harbour with evil-sounding horns blasting along the pier as the mother ship docks.

I imagine the cannons decimating the gunboats. I eagerly wait for the first three to get through the gate, the rest in military formation. I look along the line of cannons. They're in perfect position. The chakras in my body spin intensely, I rub my hands together, creating sparks. I conjure up a rapid wind through my fingertips and release the hot air along the top of the cannons. The deafening roar of the cannons creates chaos and mayhem.

In a powerful volley assault, each cannon lunges backwards, releasing its might. Eight cannonballs whizz and spin through the boiling Malta air, gaining speed as they fall to their unforeseen targets. Ear-splitting booms smash violently through the gunboats. Screams of horror erupt from the sailors as the rest of the cannonballs chop and cut the boats in half.

I hurry along the line of cannons again, shoving ball after ball into the boiling hot, smoking fronts. In round two, I conjure up the wind, and the cannons remember what they were built for—a chilling reminder of war.

Thunderous, spinning mayhem cuts through the bright blue sky as they pound again and again, tearing apart the man-made steel. Sailors leap for their lives as powerful fires roar to life, breaking out across the decks of the ships. Their comrades fall, screaming, into the rings of fire. The rest scramble desperately to escape the flames, but there's nowhere to hide from their impending doom.

The plumes of thick, black horrific smoke billow into the sky. The crunch and crash of boats come thick and fast, and the urgent shouts and screams are lost in the crackling of the flames.

A sickening blast from a gunboat below cuts through the wind, knocking me backward in slow motion. Time seems to slow down as I skid across the sharp gravel floor.

My ears ring. I shake my head to bring my eyes back into focus and jump to my feet. All I can make out through the roaring flames is a massive pileup of broken boats.

They leave the harbour in terrible carnage. Sailors bob up and down, their lifeless bodies drifting in the water. The remaining gunboats desperately try to crash through the burning fleet, but their entrance into the harbour is blocked. They are trapped out at sea, unable to make any headway.

My plan had worked a treat. The drums pounded along the harbour again, and the mother ship's Gatling guns unleashed their fury, spraying the whole terrace. I dive for cover behind the solid city walls, my ears ringing as thousands of rounds tear through the line of cannons. They turned black steel to dust in an instant. I crouch down, clutching my knees as a comfort mechanism. The hail of bullets can't breach the castle walls, but my ears are surely about to bleed. Ten minutes have passed as they unleash their hell. A never-ending spray of bullets pounds the city walls. I crouch down into a tight ball to avoid any flying shrapnel. It's a miracle they haven't hit me.

The guns spin tirelessly without ammunition, and the rotating barrels echo through the air. I jump to my feet. SAF Special forces troops are running to reload. I call on the wind, and it begins at my feet, whipping through my legs at hurricane speed, spinning violently around me.

I unleash the wind towards a huge heavy bronze bell. The military bell overlooks the harbour, and it hurtles toward the mother ship, crashing down and spinning through boat after boat, setting off a line of explosions that are the most impressive fireworks display Malta has ever seen.

Gatlin guns accidentally spin and fire at each other. Special forces are cut in half at close range. The SAF fleet, which would have caused me the most trouble, has been burned alive. Petrol flames jump angrily across the surface of the harbour, while broken pieces of leftover boats float silently in the bellowing smoke of death and destruction. Reinforcements can't get through. It's time to turn my attention to the people carriers that have made it into the harbour.

❖

CHAPTER 18

I crouch down behind a stone wall that has a perfect bird's eye view of the far end of the harbour. The people carrier boats have docked with their huge metal gates down. A thunderous vibration travels along the front and up the city walls as over one hundred horses gallop in perfect formation off the boats.

Infantrymen load up their kits and weapons, ready for their next orders. SAF special forces in full combat gear and black masks that reveal only their soulless eyes, man the Gatling guns spinning on turrets, guarding the infantry in case of another surprise attack. The tension in the air is thick and extremely dangerous. Battle drums will pound in a few hours. The proper test is yet to come as they regroup and prepare for their ground assault.

I take off, scaling up the winding cobblestone street. My legs burn within minutes as I'm met by a never-ending flight of stairs. My mind races, trying to work out which way they will attack. I conclude that the only way they can get their cavalry through the city walls is up Republic Street.

This is one of the widest and busiest streets, about half a mile long, leading to the city gate where the SAF spy fell to his death. I don't feel any remorse this time. They've trained every one of those troops to be killers with a true lust for blood. The only thing General Saturn knows is to complete his mission of destroying the One Mind and the Seal of 33 that holds the universe together.

Not on my watch. I've trained for months for this day, shedding blood, sweat, and tears to become adept in battle magic.

The never-ending stairs turn me into a sweaty mess when I reach the opening of Republic Street. It is deadly quiet. Every shop has its shutters down, and there isn't a tourist camera or walking group in sight.

The sunlight dances upon the pavement, lighting up the entire street. It must be over one hundred degrees. I reach the city gate, which is around twenty feet wide and will slow the cavalry down. This will only allow three horses through at a time, causing a bottleneck. Therefore, I set my next trap, picking them off one by one. This will surely send a message to General Saturn to rethink his steps in expanding over the sea. Finally, it will be the right time for me to return home to my family.

The main square is desolate. I take a seat at the magnificent Tritons' Fountain. The sound of the water cascading behind me puts me at ease, although I can still see angry-looking smoke in the distance over the city walls. I cross my legs and sit calmly, breathing deeply.

I focus on the sound of the water behind me, and I'm easily transported into the abyss of my mind, back to the inner world, calling for help.

'Any magician, spirit, or entity, fight with me. Show thyself, I command thee!' I raise my voice into a loud vibration one more time. "Show thyself I command thee."

I can't believe it - it's Queen Victoria.

"Sleeping on the job, are you, James?" she says as she

wanders up to the fountain.

I jump to my feet and thank her for coming.

Jean de Valette marches over to the city gate.

"James, my boy, I see it didn't take you long to spend your token. I am in your debt." He spins to the queen, bowing and spiralling his lead hand down "My liege."

The queen doesn't look happy.

"Is this it, James, the three of us? Have you been living the high life and spent all your coffers?"

I don't understand. "What do you mean, your majesty?"

Everyone I meet speaks to me in riddles. Her face scrunches up.

"In the next hour, the waiting soldiers will attack, so if you're going to war, you should have brought an army of mercenaries," she snaps.

The crunching and screeching of metal is deafening from above us. The fountain begins to shimmer with a strange mystical glow. The water bubbles and churns. The three bronze Triton statues from the fountain have awakened and are summoned for battle. I get a feeling of almighty strength bursting through my aura. They crash down in front of us ready to protect their sacred city.

"Ave, Ave, Ave," they cheer in an ancient Latin greeting.

I flash the queen a patronising grin, but she still isn't convinced.

"They will send men to strike a deal; this is where you will surrender," she barks.

Jean de Valette steps straight in.

"Nonsense, you'll have us beat before we even get into battle. Let's talk about strategy first. What is this, amateur hour?" I like Jean's confidence.

"What are we looking at, James?"

"From what I can see, one hundred cavalry horses of

well-trained men galloping off the boats in tight formation with large sabres, and to be honest, I'm not sure what could stop their charge."

This doesn't bother Jean one bit. "If you have the heart, strength, and belief you can conquer anything. We will pick them off at the city gate."

"That's the plan, Jean," I say eagerly.

We huddle together in a tight circle, and I spring straight into action, giving commands like an army general.

"OK, listen up folks," pointing down Republic Street, "the cavalry will charge directly up here. The Tritons will attack head-on, your majesty and Jean will cut them off on either side of the city gates. I will pick any of them off at the fountains."

The queen butts straight in. "This is a suicide mission." I give her a death stare and shout.

"If you're not up to the fight, then leave."

"How dare you speak to me with that forked tongue! The very insolence of you. I shall have you flogged."

I screech with laughter.

"You're from the dark ages, that shit doesn't happen anymore."

Jean roars with laughter falling about singing,

"Long live the queen, long live the queen."

The Tritons are mute as they look on eagerly, fists clenched, ready for action. The Talisman ring sparkles in the sun, and the city falls deadly quiet. There isn't a single bird in the bright blue sky.

"Take your stations, people," I shout.

The silence breaks. War drums boom from the harbour all the way up Republic Street. The beat knocks me sick, but I have to stand my ground.

A strange battle cry screeches through the microphones

in between the drums. It's all mind games to make you petrified. I levitate above the grand fountains to see what they are scheming. Their cavalry stands in precise military formation.

The frontline of the horses stamp eagerly and grunt aggressively. SAF Special forces are waiting for the call. The queen was deadly wrong. There won't be anyone striking a deal. They're only here to wipe me off the face of this earth.

Everyone waits silently. My feet land softly on the ground. A thunderous tremor travels up my legs and into my mind. I must use the Talisman ring, or we will be decimated.

The ground shakes uncontrollably with the pounding of the drums in sequence with the charging of the angry hooves. They are only a few minutes away. A cloud of dust approaches from at least one hundred bloodthirsty men.

I twirl the Talisman ring fully clockwise, then fully anticlockwise to clockwise again, vibrating the words deep in my throat and clear my mind.

"I call on thee mighty ruler of the sky, oh: RAH-ZEE-ELL! The gatekeeper to the secret angels of the universe to shine their love and light on me."

I press the red sparkling ruby with all my might. Around two hundred meters away, the cavalry is at full gallop. The drums are silenced abruptly as they tear through the city gate.

The Tritons unleash their spinning disks, whistling and hurtling through the air at an almighty speed, smashing the first line of forces to pieces. Soldier after soldier crashes off their mounts onto the unforgiving concrete.

A veil of darkness pulls across the bright blue sky. It's pitch black. My chakras spin and vibrate through my body. Divine white wings spread throughout my mind. RAH-

ZEE-ELL, with all his might, smashes to the floor. The colossal fracture in the pavement shows his boundless power. The huge, magnificent white figure stands towering before me, commanding every bit of my attention.

He looks up into the darkness and thrusts his fist at the approaching cavalry. Light breaks through the spiralling darkness, and I can't believe what I'm seeing. RAH-ZEE-ELL'S great army of seventy-two angels circle and descend from the sky at frightening speed, snatching and tearing away the SAF special forces' troops from their saddles.

Horrific screams fill the skies. I'll never forget the bloodcurdling sound of watching them plummet to their deaths. Smashing onto the rocks below, they swoop down in lines of three, picking up incredible speed with their huge, majestic wings.

Gliding above the city gate, soldiers scream off into the distance in the angels' grips. The sun breaks through the clouds as the angels hunt the last of the terrified men, swooping through the sky and snapping them in two like matchsticks.

They soar off toward the sea. There isn't a soldier in sight. All the horses, left unmanned, gallop in circles, freely surrounding the Triton fountain.

RAH-ZEE-ELL vibrates aloud. 'Shh.' The horses obey him, trotting calmly and drinking from the fountain.

The sun shines on the shadows of the angels flying out to sea. It's the most impressive sight I've ever seen. RAH-ZEE-ELL towers over me. His wings stretch out over twenty feet. He crouches down, touching the ground with his right fist, and his wings snap close. His sheer might cracks and crumbles the pavement without a word.

He blasts off, spiralling up into the heavens. The Queen and Jean applaud loudly.

"Well, we didn't expect you to have that up your sleeve!" Jean shouts.

"I thank you all for your help. Sincerely."

I jump onto the closest riderless grey horse and take off down Republic Street, the wind whipping through its beautiful mane.

I shift my weight slightly to one side and ease my foot out of the stirrup, sliding smoothly out of the saddle and dismounting the horse as I skid to a perfect stop.

After growing up on a steady diet of western movies every Saturday morning with my Uncle Crow, they secretly had an impact on me. I'm a natural in the saddle.

The last boat with the commander crashes through the pile of broken boats with an almighty crunch, making their daring escape at high speed, bouncing over the waves in defeat. General Saturn will have any of his men returning home executed for sure. They might as well be racing to their deaths.

I can't even relate to the person I was when I arrived here.

I've conquered all my fears. I've broken the chains of everyone holding me down in my life.

I am reborn, and I've mastered the great work to become a true ceremonial magician. The island of Malta will forever be in my heart.

❖

CHAPTER 19

A flock of pigeons flutters through the bustling square, stealing leftover bread from the surrounding cafes. I stroll along in my fitted beige linen suit. I'm well known in the area and always greet everyone with a smile.

The energy of the place is perfect. The sun shines brightly, lighting up the street, and there isn't a cloud in the sky. The aroma of freshly ground coffee beans greets me as I stop at my favourite corner cafe to grab an espresso.

With each sip I march off along the Birgu promenade. I have a real spring in my step, heading down the steep bank past the local church with my favourite alarm clock bells.

The local priest stands proudly in his full white robes at the entrance, holding a beautifully handcrafted white staff with a large pinecone situated at the top. His face lights up when he sees me, and we share a warm greeting.

The past few weeks have slipped through my fingers as each day has blended into the next.

I wander along the pier, and the yachts get bigger with every step. I arrive at the end, and the final one is one of the biggest vessels I've ever seen.

The huge superyacht is a sight to behold. It has garish, extravagant furnishings and multiple decks that seem to disappear diagonally into the clouds.

It's beautiful but a tad intimidating. Standing in the baking heat, I admire its sleek pearl-white front. I hear my name being shouted from above. I can't believe my eyes.

It's The Architect.

"Come on board, young man."

I run to the side and in grand writing the vessel's name is The Ark.

I bolt along the bridge, he's decked out in a suit similar to mine. With a pristine, gleaming white T-shirt, a well-groomed beard, and emerald eyes just as dazzling as the last time that I saw them.

"Wow, look at you, all dressed up and living the high life." We embrace tightly.

It's great to see him again. I whisper in his left ear,

"You need to burn those Jesus sandals, though."

"Ha-ha, I still see you have the gift of charisma."

A waiter in an immaculate white tuxedo arrives with gin and tonics and crushed ice. We relax at the stern on comfortable leather sofas.

We toast and clink our glasses together.

"I want to congratulate you on your triumphant victory. Sinking the SAF's fleet with military precision was a pleasure to watch."

I burst out laughing.

"I'm sure I was just repeating history. The Ottoman Empire fell for the same trap."

A treasure chest catches my eye, sitting in the centre of the deck, glistening in the sun. The Architect approaches the chest and says proudly,

"You are one of the most proficient magicians I have ever trained."

He strains, lifting the heavy golden lid and places

it gently onto the deck. A burst of white light shines straight up into the sky. He crouches down and lifts the hidden treasure with both hands, spinning to me with a massive grin.

"James Gunner, I award you the sacred dagger of the seal." I don't know what to say. I'm lost for words to be handed something of this magnitude. I'd heard the girls speak about it at Coven House and whomever they awarded it to was supposed to have the very power of God in their hands.

He places it into my palms, its gold glistens in the sun and it's heavy, although only about twenty centimetres long. I release the blade from its sheaf and its power surges up both my arms. It delights The Architect.

"It's with its rightful owner. You've connected with it instantly. Roll up your sleeves and look."

A beautiful, ancient Talisman tattoo appears on my arms, half on each side. "When brought together, you will activate the dagger."

The sun travels along the blade, lighting up its geometric pattern to its light blue handle. Two golden eagles hold a precious pink star diamond, wrapped in a diamond-like symbol.

"What does this symbol mean, Architect?"

"It's called a triquetra. It symbolises the eternal spiritual life, which has no beginning or end."

He loves to provoke my thoughts.

"Lift the blade to your eyes and scan from left to right. This activates the sigil to get direct contact with the archangels and harness their power."

I scan the sigil, and glorious white wings appear in my mind. The pink star diamond flashes with its almighty power, instantly giving me a sense of biblical strength.

I quickly place the blade back into its golden sheath, and the dagger's pink starlight flickers out.

"Why such a gift?"

The Architect sits next to me and explains,

"You have been awarded the dagger for travelling through the dark into your enlightenment. Many have failed before you, and it has taken true grit to get to this point in your life. You've been on a straight line to success. Well done, my son."

He continues with a warm smile, "You have one more gift."

"I love presents, keep them coming," I say eagerly.

He tosses me a set of heavy-duty keys. I recognize them straight away—it's Coven House.

"It's yours now."

I grab him and pick him up, spinning with joy.

"Thank you, thank you, Architect. When will I return home to Newcastle?"

"That is your call, James. To be honest, I thought you had taken a shine to Valletta. With your keys to Coven House, you can live like the distinguished gentleman you were always meant to be."

I don't even realise we've set sail; the yacht is so smooth, gliding along the water. We enter the grand harbour of Valletta, and there's not a burning ship in sight. Life has returned to normal.

The port is hustling and bustling with a fun holiday vibe. The super yacht cuts through wave after wave.

"James, the least I could do is give you a lift home."

We embrace again, as he bids me farewell.

I stand alone in the harbour. I have my new dagger and the keys to my new potential life in the sun. Life couldn't be better.

I walk past the many brightly coloured front doors of Malta and head to a cool bar about ten minutes' walk from the house.

The terrace offers a breathtaking view of the many surrounding historical buildings. The warmth of the sun kisses my skin as I stretch back in my seat. I find myself immersed in a haven of relaxation, just people-watching.

It's baking hot, but I must leave my suit jacket on as it's hiding the dagger in my rear belt. A friendly waiter brings my order of a large beer in a frosted glass and sets it down in front of me.

A sparkling black limousine cruises up to the entrance. Small black flags blow on the front of the bonnet, but I don't recognise the symbol. They must be diplomats.

The driver opens the rear door, and a striking-looking man gets out. He's over six feet tall, wearing an immaculately tailored suit with a ruffled black grandad-collar shirt and Cuban heels. He hides his eyes behind his shades, with high cheekbones, lean physique, and a cropped military haircut.

My eyes stay on the stranger as he glides into the bar. I can't take my eyes off him. He whistles his way through the terrace, and everyone falls silent.

I can feel the warmth of the sun on the back of my neck as he approaches my table. I get a cold shudder up my spine.

He stops directly in front of me and calmly takes out a Cuban cigar from his inside pocket, lighting it with a flash from an old-fashioned petrol lighter. A potent smell of old leather fills the air.

"Do you mind if I sit here?" He says in a deep, gravelly voice.

"Of course not, please take a seat,"

Everybody on the terrace stands up and walks off to the entrance, as though they are all in a cult-like trance. What is this black magic I am witnessing? The waiter approaches and says nothing.

He carefully places a bucket of expensive champagne and two glasses in front of the stranger. The entire bar is deadly quiet now. The man tips his head forward, revealing an anaconda tattoo spiralling up his neck in a subtle red and yellow Japanese design.

I can't put my finger on the energy I'm feeling, but it's something I've felt before here in Malta. The man turns to me and cracks a smile at the side of his bulging cigar; he removes his Ray-Bans, revealing the brightest grey-blue eyes I've ever seen.

He leans back slowly in his chair, blowing cigar smoke upwards with a gigantic sigh.

"Ah, James, you've been a busy little boy, haven't you?"

I widen my eyes to him.

"How do you know my name?"

"My watchers have followed your every move since you left England."

"Are you another SAF goon sent to assassinate me?"

He half laughs, passing me a glass of fizzing champagne.

"I work for nobody, my friend, and I'm here strictly on personal business. You've impressed me with your rise through magic and your annihilation of those imbeciles – the Shadow Advanced Federation. We could say we've met before. Let me refresh your memory for a moment, my young friend."

I push back my seat violently, reaching for the dagger at the back of my suit.

I feel scared of this man. His eyes show me a grim tale.

"Astrid," I shout. He laughs creepily again, puffing away

at his cigar and blowing circles of smoke in the air above me.

"I assure you; I mean you no harm. I'm here to offer you a deal. It's time for you to take a seat on a throne at my side and think about your bright future."

"How do you mean my future? I know who you are, but why would I choose to side with unimaginable evil?" His strange laugh fills the terrace again as he quaffs away at his champagne.

"Were you expecting a red cape and pointy horns? I come in many forms but rarely step foot on this plane."

"I'm not interested in what you're trying to sell me; you don't know where I'm from! You'd normally have a broken jaw by now."

His grin vanishes instantly, and he lunges forward, hissing like a snake at my response.

"You think I'm here to claim you, but you're wrong. I demanded that my watchers leave you alone and study you from a distance."

He takes a huge drag of his cigar and his entire demeanour changes back to being charming again.

"I am here to offer you a new contract and this will be to rule at my side. I can offer you any desire you wish."

It was hard not to listen to him as he oozed charisma.

"This is our time, and I have nearly won. Man does not care about his fellow man. I've hypnotised so many mortals as they drift through their lives. I can see you have great potential. You woke up. What magnificent pain we could create together with you as my portal. We will release pure and utter chaos to this realm. Don't you want to live forever at the age you are right now?"

"I'm sorry, I'm not interested in your offer." Slowly edging backwards, he's giving me the total creeps now.

I reach around slowly, gripping the dagger hard.

"Ah," he sighs, "The Architect's dagger is now in your grasp. I know he's been here today. I can smell his stench of holiness and look at what he's brought you – an antique flashy dagger that should be in an Egyptian museum."

He calmly stands, buttons his suit jacket back up, knocks back the rest of his champagne, then looks at me dead in the eyes.

"So then, Mr. Gunner, what will your answer be? I have many souls to collect today from binding contracts."

"I'm going to have to decline your offer and ask you to leave me alone." He sniggers and spins on one heel. Looking over his shoulder he shouts back.

"Have fun shining your dagger."

He glides off in cigar smoke, whistling the tune *Jealous Guy* by John Lennon. As soon as he steps back into his limousine, the bar fills back up in an instant.

It's as though he stopped time to offer me his new contract. I feel confused and can't work out why everyone wants a piece of me. I can't imagine that creep coming for you when your time's up. I leave a twenty euro note for my beer and take off along the stunning winding streets of lower Valletta.

❖

CHAPTER 20

I arrive at Coven House, I've missed the canary yellow door of my newly owned establishment.

To my surprise, I find the door unlocked. I can hear a noise on the top floor.

I sprint up the spiral staircase, two flights. Pizza boxes are piled high and empty wine bottles are scattered along the kitchen top. I reach the top floor, and I'm stopped in my tracks.

It's Sky. I feel my eyes well up. She looks stunning, as always, with her dark chocolate perfect skin. She stands so elegantly, her pink and yellow sari dancing in the wind from the terrace. She is a sight to behold.

"James!" she screams, diving on top of me, sobbing nonstop.

"Where the hell have you been? I thought you'd been killed." I wipe away her tears and stare into her deep beautiful eyes.

"I thought Layla betrayed me and set a trap with The SAF. I've been hiding in a safe house in Birgu for months."

She wipes away the rest of the tears on her rosy cheeks.

"What's wrong?"

"Layla's dead." I couldn't believe what I was hearing.

"How?"

"She was found last month in her London apartment. She was naked, lying outside her protective circle. Every bone in her body was broken, and whoever killed her contorted her head backwards." Sky started sobbing uncontrollably again. "I don't think I'll ever get over it. I loved her like a sister. It's ripped my heart out."

I felt numb inside hearing the grim news.

I hugged Sky tightly and whispered,

"It's all over now, as long as you're okay."

I knew deep in my heart that Astrid had tricked her into stepping outside of her circle.

"She just went back to London in a huff because she couldn't handle it when you took the limelight."

I noticed two suitcases in the lobby.

"Where are you going?"

She stepped back, concern written across her face.

"Perfect timing. You idiot, the car's on its way to take me to the airport. It's time for me to head back to New York."

"Don't go!" I blurted out.

"I have to. I promised my family." She stared at me in disbelief.

"Why don't you move to New York?" She sprang toward me. "Put all of this behind you. My folks have a property in Manhattan. We can start a life together. You know I love you."

I understood my basic need for love. Could I make this work without messing it up? I gazed into her eyes, reading her desperation for me to say yes. But just as the moment hung in the air, a taxi horn beeped loudly outside, spoiling everything. I clambered up, breaking the spell. "I'm sorry I need more time to think this through."

She kisses me gently on the lips and whispers.

"You've got two weeks. I won't wait forever."

She skips down the stairs with her magical youthful energy. The driver had already loaded her cases. I raced down after her, standing on the pavement, watching as she slipped away. A sinking feeling hit the pit of my stomach as she glanced back at me through the rear-view mirror. I couldn't shake the sense of loss. There were too many questions I didn't have the answers to, but to be honest, I'd bottled it.

I turned and headed up to The Wheelhouse, fixing a drink to calm my nerves.

A few hours passed, and I just stared off into a daze, watching the busy harbour. I found myself contemplating Sky's proposal—life in New York, a wedding in Central Park, and a reception at the boathouse. It sounded appealing, and Sky would be a beautiful bride.

I've always loved New York. But the million-dollar question lingered—could I really settle down and get married?

I missed the views up here. From the terraces, the sight of the city was breathtaking. I'd sleep on it, spend the night on the terrace, and hope the stars might offer me some clarity.

❖

CHAPTER 21

I had settled into my perfect little new life. I was back on top form and fighting fit. Thirty days had passed since I'd started my new healthy regime. No alcohol, clean eating, and exercising twice a day. But I felt like I was running against the clock. Sky was never off the phone begging me to go to the States.

I had come to appreciate every moment at Coven House and was dragging my feet.

It's a fabulous morning up at The Wheelhouse and the city is alive. I'm awake early, squinting up at the sky.

The news headlines caught my eye.

I quickly dive for the remote, switching on the TV. In bold red writing scrolling along the bottom of the screen: *Terrorist cell captured in Northern England.*

My heart stopped, and my brain couldn't comprehend the words. Someone had given my whole family up. I was looking at my auntie's house and my dad, Uncle Crow, and grandad were on their knees, handcuffed behind their backs.

It looked like The SAF were preparing for a mass execution. I need to keep my cool, knowing its all theatre - television propaganda designed to rule with fear.

General Saturn appears on the screen wearing a black

beret and full military camouflage, with a smug expression on his face.

He begins his statement.

"We are thrilled with the intelligence we have received, resulting in the capture of the Gunner family. A dawn raid has successfully destroyed their terrorist cell. We are interested in one more fugitive, Mr. James Gunner, whom we believe is on the run overseas. He is to be considered highly dangerous and should not be approached."

The interviewer interrupts General Saturn.

"What will happen to the men you have captured today?"

Putting him on the spot, he pauses for a moment, not used to being challenged due to his insane ego. He stares directly into the screen with his dead eyes.

"They will be tried for high treason. If found guilty, they will be hung from the Tyne Bridge as an example to all Northerners."

The breaking news disappears from the screen, and I'm left stunned. I am aware of the catastrophic consequences of my return home, but I cannot stand by and watch my family get hurt.

I march over to the bar and release the dagger from its sheath, running my eyes along the geometric sigil and clashing the insides of my arms together, vibrating the activating words deeply in my throat.

The Architect is called to come to me. I know he will know what to do.

A golden portal crackles in the air, the edges hum with electricity and spark with dangerous energy as it opens six feet high at the side of the rooftop bar.

The Architect steps though, and I blast him immediately with my dilemma.

"The SAF has captured my family at my auntie's safe house. I don't understand. It's in the middle of nowhere. Someone had to have betrayed them."

The Architect clicks his fingers with a golden blast, and he draws a circle through the very fabric of the air to reveal the traitor.

My heart sinks as it shows Ethan accepting a vast sum of money from Crowley Saturn. I should have known and followed the dots. With Ethan's debts to The Crow and spiralling drug habit, he would be the first person to betray us."That shit house," I scream, "he's dead to me."

He'll snort that money and piss the rest away up the wall in less than a year. My chakras spin violently in my body. The sheer force knocks The Architect back. I can't control them. The anger charges up my spine and white light bursts out from my eyes.

The Architect raises his voice to control the beast within.

"James, calm yourself."

He brings my eyes back into focus, and I compose myself again. I turn to him, looking for any pearls of wisdom.

In an assertive tone, he speaks.

"You know what to do. Follow your heart. This is your ultimate test. Return home with your training and set your family free. It's time to smash The SAF and break its back. A boat named Freya will wait for you at 7 p.m. tonight at the marina to take you on your voyage home. Good luck, and God speed."

He vanished into another portal. I quickly grabbed my burner phone. Luckily, I remembered my dad's number by heart. It rang.

"Dad. Is that you?" The line was silent. An evil chuckle echoed down the line.

"I had a sneaky feeling you'd ring daddy's phone after the news report." It's Amora.

"You heartless bitch," I snap back.

"What will it be, James? Are you manning up?"

"If you release my whole family, you can take me into custody."

There's a long silence.

"OK, trade yourself in and all of this will be over for your family. I will release them at the time of your arrest. You have my word."

"OK, I will arrive at Tynemouth Long Sands Beach by boat. I'll see you in exactly twenty-four hours."

The shock of the call caused my hands to tremble, my phone slipped from my grip and crashed onto the bar.

I couldn't shake the feeling that everything had changed in an instant. It took a few hours to calm myself down, packing an overnight bag of clothes. I locked the large canary yellow door behind me. "Wish me luck," I murmured to the seahorse knocker in the centre.

I made my way through the harbour, and as 7 p.m. approached, I was right on time. I spotted a magnificent yacht with gold calligraphy along the side: Freya. And look who's manning the ship—Captain Sid.

"Ahoy, Jim, lad!" Captain Sid shouts from the top deck as I dash across the bridge and onto the boat. He pulls me into a powerful hug, slapping my back hard.

I laugh out loud, saying, "You've got an upgrade, you crafty bugger."

"I know! I couldn't believe it when The Coven came through, and now I've ended up with this beauty. My instructions are to deliver you to Newcastle?"

"Yes, Tynemouth Long Sands," I reply.

"Alright, we've got fantastic facilities on board. Your

voyage home will be smooth, and before you know it, you'll be back in God's country. This yacht can handle any weather, and your safety is paramount."

I thank him and go for a look around.

This beats fish guts and machine-gun bullets flying along the deck any day. The evening air carries a slight chill. My body feels exhausted as we head east on our voyage. So, I head below deck for some rest.

Captain Sid navigated Freya under the new moonlight charging across the sea. I was taken aback by my luxurious bedroom. The space was beautiful, with a large, comfortable round bed, and a huge, old wooden ship's wheel above it. The walls are lined with elegant artwork, leading me through to the en-suite, where a marble bathtub stood proudly in the centre of the bathroom.

I look out the port-side windows, watching as wave after wave rolled away. Malta slowly disappearing in the distance, becoming a tiny, perfect rock.

❖

CHAPTER 22

MY eyes flash open, and I spring off the bed. We had arrived in the North of England. I could feel it in my bones. Darting up the stairs to the deck, I lock eyes with Captain Sid, but neither of us speaks as we approach Long Sands Beach. A sense of dread settles in my stomach. It feels like a trap.

It's an eerie Halloween night, with the full moon dominating the sky. It's like a bright biblical disc that lights up the outlines of crowds on the beach.

"Get yourself ready," Captain Sid says firmly.

The dagger is hidden in the back of my jeans. I take a step back, scanning the geometric pattern along the blade from left to right as I vibrate the words.

"I call on all angels in the north and the heavens: As above, so below to protect me." Energy soars from the tips of my toes to the top of my head. The chakras in my body spin violently.

I jam the dagger back into its sheaf. I know I've made contact. All I have to do now is wait and hope they answer my prayer.

The boat suddenly comes to a violent halt.

Captain Sid releases the anchor with a deafening clank,

and slowly, steadily, the heavy chain descends, securing Freya into position.

"It's time to put an end to these lunatics, Jim," Captain Sid says.

I hug him quickly and take off along the deck to the rear of the boat. I dive into the inflatable speedboat and ignite its small, powerful engine.

I spin away to the left of Freya at frightening speed, jumping across wave after wave. The speedboat surges forward, leaving the imposing silhouette of Freya behind.

I follow my heart, and it leads me to Long Sands Beach. The waves part before me, but there's no hiding from the bitter cold of the North Sea. My nose runs constantly. The sprays of water sting my eyes like tiny hellraiser needles.

As I approach the shore, I watch in despair. The whole stretch of the beach reveals a cavalry of about one hundred horses. Their breath forms icy plumes in the freezing night air. Their mighty hooves shift the damp, wet sand as they wait to charge, dressed in battle gear, armed to the teeth, mounted by General Saturn's best men.

To the right, ten black and grey camouflage Hummer vehicles stand in formation, their loud engines rumbling along the sand, their blue lights spinning and flashing. The guards grip heavy automatic weapons, all pointing in my direction.

I can just make out my dad, Uncle Crow, and my grandad, all on their knees with their hands tied behind their backs, their faces pushed into the freezing sand.

Ethan stands to the right of General Saturn, Amora, Crowley, and heavily armed bodyguards.

The North Sea's freezing water sprays my face one last time. I grit my teeth as I catch the last enormous wave and skid to a violent stop on the sand.

Thundering hooves approach, galloping up a mist of damp sand from a small group of SAF special forces troops. Without a word spoken, I'm marched up the beach by his goons towards General Saturn and his small waiting army. My feet sink deeply into the wet sand with every step, my legs turn to lead.

I'm ten metres away and Ethan looks petrified. He can't look me in the eye because of his betrayal. The colour drains from his face. He just hangs his head in shame, like a complete loser.

I give General Saturn a death stare and don't break eye contact, showing him, I have no fear. Ethan looks at me and whispers a silent "Sorry."

General Saturn smiles and says,

"Welcome home, Mr. Gunner." His hand moves with real purpose, slipping inside his dark green military jacket, quickly drawing a pistol, and crashing it into Ethan's temple with a deafening bang.

He falls lifelessly onto the blood-soaked sand beneath him. Time seemed to slow down, and my eyes went out of focus. I couldn't believe I'd just witnessed my best friend being executed.

"Did you hear me?" General Saturn screams in my face. "It's time for you and your family to die on this beach tonight."

He calmly says, "I will look forward to the Halloween massacre of the Gunner family."

Roaring with laughter, he spins and marches away to Amora. "You know what to do!" He commands.

The Crow catches my eye and gives me a nod and reassuring smile. I knew he would have something up his sleeve. Suddenly, I hear glorious music travelling across the beach. The chanter of Scottish bagpipes dances in the wind and highland snare drums rhythmically buzz towards us.

Over two hundred magical men approach in full, striking red tartan kilts. It's The Crow's backup – the McAllister clan from Inverness and Glencoe. That's my cue.

I close my eyes and tap into my telepathic powers. I whisper to the SAF cavalry horses.

"I call on thee my beauties. Free yourselves from these evil men on your backs." The horses grunt and spin in circles nervously. I scream at the top of my voice, "Free yourselves."

They gallop at speed, charging into the water, catapulting the troops one by one into the freezing waves. This leaves a huge opening at the north end of the beach. All hell breaks loose as a massive surge of the McAllister clan charges.

Troops fall helplessly from their horses as the clan let out their war cry, drawing their blades, and releasing their axes, chopping through General Saturn's disorganised troops. The fierce, deadly assault breaks the confidence of the men trying to get back out of the rough sea and onto the sand. I quickly free everyone's cable ties, slicing them with my dagger, and we dive for cover into a nearby dune.

White bolts of lightning screech through the night sky and whizz past our heads. Magical bolts ignite from the clan's bagpipes, decimating the special forces troops. The powerful hands of my dad grab my shoulder, holding me back.

"Wait for it, wait for it, son," he whispers.

Uncle Crow sets the pace as we scramble and claw our way out of the dunes and straight into battle.

General Saturn runs toward me, two of his goons by his side, a panicked look on his face as he screams, "Kill them! Kill them!"

I duck down, and a screaming bolt of lightning screeches past my head. A sudden, chilling shriek travels along the sand. I spin and look. The bolt of lightning strikes the General. The force of the impact throws him to the sand. He's holding onto his burning face in agony, the synthetic muscles and tendons under his skin begin to twitch and contort. His right eye dangles from a shiny mechanical socket.

Everything is falling into place now. All I had to do was follow the dots. How could a human lack so much empathy? All along, he was a machine hidden in plain sight.

Amora skids in the sand like an Olympic long jumper, looking at her father in horror.

The SAF's Hummer vehicles approach at high speed from the rear, opening fire. Deafening heavy artillery cuts across the sand, chopping some of the clan in half. The strangest thing happens. I see angel wings in the third eye of my mind.

I look up at the dark sky overhead. It is suddenly pitch black. A gigantic shadow looms along Long Sands Beach. It floats silently, spiralling down toward us.

The North's hearts and souls are protected by a bronze, rusty giant sculpture with a wingspan of over fifty metres. The Angel of the North crashes into the sand behind us, sending an earthquake rupturing along the beach, violently knocking everyone off their feet.

We all jump back to our feet, confused. I think, by the look on the faces of the troops, they all know they were going to die as they run, screaming for their lives. The Hummer vehicles skid to a stop and reverse rapidly away. Their tyres spin uncontrollably in the sand, but they're going nowhere fast, sinking every second.

The Angel lunges at them, crashing its wings into the side of several vehicles, catapulting them toward the sea. The trucks are battered and crushed by the deafening impact as steel meets steel.

The SAF's troops' terror grows rapidly as they run for cover, for the Angel plays a sadistic game of cat and mouse, stamping every one of them into the sand in a horrific explosion of blood. The last of the disorganised troops don't stand a chance.

The Angel of the North kneels beside the smoking wreckage, giving me a silent nod as it soars off into the moonlight.

Crowley appears from behind the angry black billowing smoke, glaring at me with extreme rage, screaming.

"You're dead Gunner." He approaches me thick and fast.

I quickly close the gap between us but forget I still have the dagger in my hand. The clown trips over his own feet and falls heavily onto the dagger, slashing his face from corner to corner. He falls into the sand, screaming in pain, holding onto his peeling flesh.

I quickly grab for the dagger and slip it back into my belt. Suddenly, I see Amora sprinting through the flames and smoke, she jumps four feet off the sand with a spinning roundhouse kick. Her tactical leather boots stamp deep into my chest, and we fly backwards into the freezing water.

The current is swift and deadly. Amora carries on with her attack, punching me nonstop, each impact like a sledgehammer against my chin. I struggle to defend myself until we both get swept away down the beach. I spring out of a large, freezing wave, and she catches me again with a perfect punch in her leather gloves.

She hits me again with a flying elbow and it echoes in my ears and down my spine. She's relentless. I'm going to have to drown this bitch.

She grabs me by the scruff of the neck. At first, I thought she was going to take a chunk out of my cheek.

"Listen to me, James, you need to destroy The Hive. It's hidden somewhere outside the country, only a few people know about it. I'll try to get you to the location once all of this has died down. Destroy it and break the grid, and you will defeat my father—or whatever he is. Please end this madness!"

A powerful wave crashes over our heads with a deafening roar. I struggle to regain my footing, and panic sets in. I cling to her hand in desperation as thoughts of drowning race through my mind.

We both burst out of the water, gasping for breath. My chest heaves as I fight desperately to fill my lungs with oxygen.

I brush Amora's wet hair from her face with one hand, clinging to the other. I look deeply at her; she shakes her head and spins away to shield her eyes. There is a glimpse of the real Amora.

"We don't have time for this, James. Maybe in another life, we could have been something."

I've broken the ice queen. We bob up and down, our freezing lips suddenly clashing together passionately.

She pulls back. "James, I will find you. Please let me escape to my father's submarine. I'll say you've been swept away and drowned."

As my hand releases her grip, all I can do is hope she reaches the submarine before hypothermia sets in.

She bursts into an aggressive front crawl, swimming in the opposite direction of the beach. I scramble out of the freezing water. Amora is long gone. I take off jogging back along the beach, shivering from head to toe with every foot that plunges into the damp sand. I pick up my pace, the beach is one deadly sight to see.

Every vehicle is destroyed in a hail of fire and billowing smoke. The cries of death have been silenced. A huge, happy herd of unmanned military horses gallop past me to their freedom. There isn't a soul around as I slow down and walk through great clouds of smoke that sweep across the beach. It's hard to make out if any of The SAF's troops have survived, but I doubt it.

I look down with a heavy heart as Ethan's remains have turned to burned ash from the battle. My best friend's soul is taken through his addiction and betrayal, leaving a bitter taste in my mouth. A frozen tear slides down my cheek.

I quickly start up one of the leftover military jeeps and dive into the driver's seat, taking off at high speed, racing into the night through North Tyneside, punching the steering wheel with joy. We did it; we conquered and broke The SAF's back. Twenty minutes later, I spin the wheels up Byker Bank and cruise along The Quayside.

The river is deadly quiet. Every SAF boat has disappeared.

The only thing left is their flags, flying defeated in the wind.

I skid the vehicle to a halt outside The Oyster Soul and burst through the double swinging doors to a scene that looks like Valhalla. The whole restaurant is jam-packed with the McAllister clan.

Heavy wooden tables line the room and screams of laughter and joy fill the air. The Jocks know how to have a good time, I have a sneaky feeling they will drink the bar dry in a few hours.

My dad, grandad, and Uncle Crow stand propping up the bar. All their faces light up with amazement. I crash into them with roars of laughter.

"We beat the bastards," my dad shouts, looking the happiest I've ever seen him. His face looks ten years younger as he laughs and jokes with his dad and brother.

"Here, son," he says, throwing me a set of keys.

"What are these?"

"It's the keys to the castle." I'm a bit confused.

"Meaning?"

"You're the gaffer now. I'm retiring." I can't believe it.

"I never thought you'd give up the throne to the Gunner empire."

"I'm done, young'un. I'm off to live in the sun with your mam."

Duncan interrupts the whole restaurant, banging on the microphone. We all listen intently.

"Hello, everyone. I'd like to say a special thanks to the Gunner family and the McAllister clan for today's valiant efforts. Their unbelievable courage carried them to triumph. We have all battled and accomplished something truly remarkable, defeating the evil that tried to take away our very way of life. Magic has always been in our hearts and will forever be the sleeping giant in the North. We have won the battle but not the war, so don't let your guard down. The clan will stay on at the borders in Berwick, and Newcastle is back in the hands of its proud people. Let us raise our glasses to all the men and women we lost today."

The whole place erupts with a deafening roar of the magical clan as they clash their glasses and cheer to our victory.

I take a moment to myself to wander out onto the terrace. I'm home, and a sense of peace washes over me. I take a deep breath, inhaling the cool, fresh air. Duncan's words still haunt me and linger in the night air.

We have won the battle but not the war.

Printed in Dunstable, United Kingdom

75090682R00102